"What an

"You." He th[...]
scent of her[...]
hit him like t[...]

He was going about this all wrong. Staying away from her in order to keep her made no sense at all.

He needed to get closer.

Closer. Dear God. He would love that.

Too bad he was no good at all that love and romance crap. And if he went for it with Elise and it blew up In his face, where would he be then? Zero and two—*and* minus the assistant who made it all hang together.

"Jed." She'd reached the table and now stood over him, watching him, her smile indulgent, her eyes so bright. "What's going on in that big brain of yours?"

"Not a thing."

"Liar. You've got your scary face on—give me your plate. I'll warm it up."

He handed it over. He watched her walk away. Always a pleasure, watching Elise walk away.

What would it be like, him and Elise, living together, working together, sleeping in the same bed night after night? He was starting to think he really needed to find out.

THE BRAVOS OF JUSTICE CREEK:
Where bold hearts collide under Western skies

Dear Reader,

Elise Bravo needs a high-paying job to put herself back on track after a series of losses in life, in business and in love. Jed Walsh needs the perfect assistant. He's a world-famous thriller writer with a specific writing process: he dictates his stories to his assistant. Unfortunately, Jed is big and gruff and scary, a real beast of a man. He's having serious trouble keeping a typist; they tend to run away screaming.

And then Elise shows up at Jed's door to apply for the job no other assistant has been able to keep. She's a whiz on the keyboard and he doesn't intimidate her. Jed may be hard to deal with, but he pays a lot.

It's only supposed to be a temporary solution. She'll type his overdue book, make all that money and go back to her own life.

But then slowly, Elise begins to realize that she's falling for her secretly softhearted beast of a boss. As for Jed, he's decided that, no matter what it takes or how much it costs him, he's never letting Elise go...

I hope you enjoy their story as much as I did.

Happy reading, everyone.

Christine Rimmer

Ms. Bravo
and the Boss

———

Christine Rimmer

⬧HARLEQUIN® SPECIAL EDITION®

Recycling programs
for this product may
not exist in your area.

ISBN-13: 978-0-373-65985-2

Ms. Bravo and the Boss

Printed in U.S.A.

Christine Rimmer came to her profession the long way around. She tried everything from acting to teaching to telephone sales. Now she's finally found work that suits her perfectly. She insists she never had a problem keeping a job—she was merely gaining "life experience" for her future as a novelist. Christine lives with her family in Oregon. Visit her at christinerimmer.com.

Books by Christine Rimmer

Harlequin Special Edition

The Bravos of Justice Creek

James Bravo's Shotgun Bride
Carter Bravo's Christmas Bride
The Good Girl's Second Chance
Not Quite Married

The Bravo Royales

A Bravo Christmas Wedding
The Earl's Pregnant Bride
The Prince's Cinderella Bride
Holiday Royale
How to Marry a Princess
Her Highness and the Bodyguard
The Rancher's Christmas Princess

Bravo Family Ties

A Bravo Homecoming
Marriage, Bravo Style!
Donovan's Child
Expecting the Boss's Baby

Montana Mavericks: What Happened at the Wedding?

The Maverick's Accidental Bride

Montana Mavericks: 20 Years in the Saddle!

Million-Dollar Maverick

Visit the Author Profile page
at Harlequin.com for more titles.

For Nalria Wisdom Gaddy,
who knows the names of all the flowers
and never fails to brighten my day.
Nalria, this one's for you.

Chapter One

Elise Bravo wanted a bath. A long, relaxing one. With lots of bubbles. She longed to shed every stitch and pile her hair up on her head. To grab a juicy paperback romance and sink into her slipper tub, the one she'd had specially installed in the big master bath of her two-bedroom apartment above her catering shop in the gorgeous old brick building she co-owned with her best friend, Tracy.

Unfortunately, Elise's beautiful slipper tub was no more. Neither was her apartment. Her business? Gone, too. Three months ago, the historic building on Central Street in her hometown of Justice Creek, Colorado, had burned to the ground.

As for her lifelong best friend? Tracy had moved to Seattle to start a whole new life.

Now, Elise lived in a tiny rented studio apartment

over Deeliteful Donuts on the less attractive end of Creekside Drive. The studio had a postage stamp of a bathroom—with a shower, no tub.

And sometimes lately, as she raced through the lunch rush at her sister Clara's café, or manned the counter at her half sister Jody's flower shop, Elise could almost lose heart. She was deeply disappointed in herself.

Because it wasn't the fire that had ruined her life. She'd been in trouble long before the idiot tenants who leased a shop on the ground floor had disabled the fire alarms and then left a hot plate turned on in the back room when they slipped out to run errands. By then, bad choices had already brought Elise to the brink of ruin. The fire had only slathered a thick helping of frosting on her own personal disaster cake.

Elise was one of four siblings. She had five half siblings. Of the nine children of Franklin Bravo, Elise was the only one who'd blown through her very generous inheritance. Shame dogged her for every one of her stupid choices in life, in love and in business. She was circling the drain and she didn't really know what to do about it.

Except to hold her head high, work hard and keep moving forward.

After the lunch rush at the Library Café on that fateful day in June, Elise took off her waitress apron and transferred her tips to her purse. Her sister Clara waved at her as she went out the back door.

It was a warm, sunny day. Elise had walked to the café. Now, she set out on foot along Central Street headed for Jody's shop, Bloom. It was good exercise, walking. Not to mention, it saved on gas. Walking fast, she could reach Bloom in six minutes and be right on time to give Jody a break at two o'clock.

She made it with a minute to spare. Jody, at the counter with a customer, glanced over at the sound of the bell. "There you are."

"What? Am I late? I thought we said—"

"You're not late," said a voice to Elise's left. She whipped her head around in surprise as her other half sister popped out from behind a ficus tree and grabbed Elise's arm. "We need to talk."

"What the…?" Elise tried to jerk free. "Nell! Let me go."

But Nell, who worked in construction, had a grip like a sumo wrestler. "Come on in back."

Elise sent Jody a pleading look as Nell dragged her toward the swinging café doors on the far side of the counter. "Jody, will you tell her to let go of—"

"Hear her out," Jody interrupted. She was tucking a stunning arrangement of succulents and red anthuriums into one of Bloom's trademark green-and-pink boxes. "This could be good for you."

"This? What?" Elise huffed in frustration as Nell knocked the doors wide and dragged Elise into the back room. "Will someone please tell me what's going on?"

"This way." Nell pulled her into Jody's office and shut the door. "Sit."

Elise plunked her purse on Jody's desk. "This is ridiculous."

"Just sit down and listen."

"Fine." Elise dropped into the guest chair. "But Jody has errands to run and she needs me out front."

"Don't worry about Jody. She'll manage without

you." Nell braced a hip against the desk and crossed her arms over her spectacular breasts.

Actually, Nell was spectacular all over. She had legs for days and long, thick auburn hair and lips like Angelina Jolie. A half sleeve of gorgeous ink accentuated her shapely left arm. Elise, on the other hand, possessed neither the style nor the courage to get a tattoo. She had dark brown hair, ordinary lips and a body that was heavier than it used to be due to some serious stress eating since the fire. Really, how could she and the gorgeous creature in front of her possibly share half of the same genes?

Elise and Nell had a difficult history. Recently, they'd healed the old wounds. But Elise still felt guilty about the way she'd treated Nell when Nell's mother married their father. And lately, with all that had gone wrong in Elise's life, the guilt was worse than ever. Now, she looked back on her earlier sense of entitlement and verging-on-mean-girl behavior and couldn't help wondering if she deserved the hard knocks she kept taking.

Still. Nellie had no right to go dragging her all over the place.

Elise folded her own arms tight and hard to match her sister's pose and demanded, "All right, I'm listening. What do you just *have* to talk to me about?"

Nell tossed her glorious hair. "A job, that's what. A lot better job than busting your butt waiting tables for Clara and running the register for Jody."

"What job?" Elise tried to stay pissed off, mostly in order not to get her hopes up. But still, she could feel it. A sudden pulse of optimism, a lifting sensation under her ribs. She used to love it when she got that feeling. Not anymore. Lately, hope only led to disappointment.

She'd had way more than enough of that already, thank you very much.

Nell uncrossed her arms and hitched a long jean-clad leg up on the desk. "This is the deal. Jed Walsh is in need of another assistant." Jed Walsh, so the story went, had grown up in a one-room cabin on a mountain not far from Justice Creek. He'd moved away right out of high school, eventually becoming the world-famous author of a series of bestselling adventure novels. Several months ago, he'd come back to town.

And yep. There it was. The sinking sensation that came when each new hope was dashed. "Of course Jed Walsh needs a new assistant. He always needs a new assistant. How many has he been through now?" Since his return to town, Walsh's inability to keep an assistant had become downright legendary.

"Don't be negative," her sister muttered.

"Nellie. They run away screaming. He's that bad."

"Let me finish. I was at Walsh's house an hour ago switching out custom hardware and—"

"What are you doing switching out hardware?"

"Stop changing the subject." Nell worked with their brother Garrett running Bravo Construction. They'd built Walsh's new house.

"But switching out hardware is way below your pay grade."

"If you must know, when Jed Walsh wants a tweak or an upgrade, I handle it. He can be annoying and I don't want him giving our people any crap. And *because* I was just there at his house, I heard him fire the woman he hired a few days ago." She leaned toward Elise. "I know you can type, Leesie. I remember you took keyboarding class back in high school and Mrs. Clemo kissed your ass because you were so good at it."

"So what? I hate typing."

"Yeah, maybe. But you can do it and do it well. And that's what Jed Walsh needs. Someone to type his book while he dictates it. The man pays big bucks."

"Come on. No one ever lasts. They all say he's a slave driver. And just possibly borderline insane. I've heard the stories. He terrorizes them. Seriously, why would I last when no one else has?"

"Because it's a lot of money."

"Not if I run away screaming, it's not."

"You're not running anywhere. You'll be the one who lasts."

"And you say that because…?"

"You're motivated. And deep down, where it counts, you're as tough as they come."

"Thanks. But no thanks." Elise reached for her purse.

Nell got to it first. She shoved it away to the center of the desk.

"Enough now, I mean it." Elise rose. "Cut it out."

"Please stop." Nell looked straight in her eyes and spoke with heartfelt intensity. "Come on, Leesie. Give up the act. You need the money and you need it bad. Stop pretending you don't."

Elise realized her mouth was hanging open and snapped it shut. She'd been so sure that nobody knew the extent of her problem. She sank back into the chair and hung her head. "Just tell me. Please. Does everybody in the family know?" Silence from Nell. Elise made herself lift her head and pull her shoulders up straight. "Do they?"

Slowly, Nell nodded. "We love you and we are not

blind. You're working yourself into the ground. And if you had the money, you would have reopened Bravo Catering when the insurance paid out." She would have, it was true. But half of that money had been Tracy's and Tracy had finally admitted that the catering business wasn't for her. Plus, Elise had had all those debts to pay. In the end, they'd split the insurance money and sold the lot to a merchant next door who wanted to expand. Once Elise had paid off what she owed, there wasn't much left. Nell went on, "That's why you need to go see Jed Walsh. Leesie, we are talking thousands a week if you can last."

"Oh, come on. Thousands? For a secretary?"

"The woman he just fired said so. I asked her as she was stomping out the door."

"She must have been exaggerating. If he pays thousands, someone would have stayed."

"No. I think he's actually *that* bad. And he's evidently damn picky. Most of them he fires, so they can't stick no matter how much they want the money he's paying. But the good news is, he's really desperate now. I heard he's blown off his book deadline over and over. At some point he's got to keep an assistant and get the damn book done."

Elise sighed in defeat. "Be realistic. If none of the others can put up with him, what makes you think *I* can?"

"Because you're a Bravo and a Bravo gets out there and gets it done." Nell stood. "Jed Walsh is going to get the assistant he needs, which is you. And that means Jed Walsh is going to put *you* back in the black."

"Oh, I doubt that."

Nell braced her hands on her shapely hips. "You

know, Leesie… On second thought, you're right. You should just give up now. We all love you and we're all doing great financially. We can help and we will. No one's going to hold it against you if you let your family rescue you from the consequences of your own stupid pride and bad decision-making."

Elise rose again, slowly. She said in a low voice that sounded like a threatening growl, "No. Freaking. Way. I'll rescue myself, just you watch me."

A slow grin tipped the corners of Nell's impossibly sexy lips. "That's the spirit." She grabbed a square of paper from the pad on the desk and bent to scribble on it. Then she took Elise's hand and slapped the paper in it. "Here's the address. Now get over there and show Mr. Number One *New York Times* Bestselling Author that you're the assistant he's been looking for."

Walsh's new house was really something, Elise thought. Bravo Construction must be proud. Surrounded by giant pines and Douglas firs, the gorgeous, rustic, wood-and-stone home sprawled impressively on the crest of a hill.

I really, truly do not want to do this, Elise repeated to herself for the hundredth time as she parked her SUV in front of the slate walk that meandered upward toward the massive front door. Excuses scrolled through her mind: She really should at least have called first. Her typing was rusty. She hated to be shouted at and everyone said that Walsh was a yeller.

But then again, her family *knew*. She could no longer lie to herself that her abject failure to take care of herself and her future was her own little secret. They knew and they worried for her and if she didn't pull herself out of this hole she was in, they would do it for her.

Uh-uh. No way. Not going to happen. *She'd* dug this hole and then fallen into it. One way or another, she would get *herself* out of it. If there was any possibility that Jed Walsh might provide the solution she'd so desperately been seeking, she needed to convince the madman to hire her.

Elise smoothed her hair, straightened her white button-down shirt and put one foot in front of the other all the way up the winding stone walk. The front porch was really something, made of rough-hewn rock and thick unfinished planks cut from various exotic-looking woods. The studded door had copper sculptures of leaves and vines attached to the windows on either side. No doorbell, just a giant cast-iron boar's-head knocker.

Elise lifted the knocker and banged it three times against the door. The thing was loud. She could hear the sound echoing on the other side. She waited for a full count of twenty for someone to answer. When no one did, she lifted the ring through the boar's snout to knock again.

Before she could lower it, the big door swung inward.

And there stood Jed Walsh, a giant of a man in jeans and a black T-shirt with muscles on his muscles, a scruff of beard on his rocklike jaw and a phone at his ear.

He shouted into the phone, "I don't care about any of that, Holly. She didn't work out and I need someone else *now*." The person on the other end started talking. Walsh pulled the phone from his ear and looked Elise up and down with a way-too-observant pair of icy green eyes. "Who are you and what do you want?"

"I'm Elise Bravo and—"

"With the construction company?" he barked. "The hardware's great and I'm happy with the copper sink. No problems." He started to swing the door shut in her face.

Elise talked fast. "You need an assistant and I'm here for the job."

He grunted, swung the door wide once more and spoke into the phone again. "Never mind for now." Whoever Holly was, she was still talking as he disconnected the call. And Walsh was giving Elise another leisurely once-over, from the top of her head to the toes of her practical black shoes.

The look was way too assessing. Please. The last thing she needed right now was to have some man— any man, crazy or otherwise—looking her over. She was not at her best, all frazzled and tired, with the buttons down the front of her shirt on the verge of popping and her black pants clinging tighter than they ought to. She was an excellent cook, after all. Plus, there was the donut shop right downstairs from her cramped apartment. Food could offer great comfort when your world went up in flames.

And then again, so what if he ogled her? She hitched up her chin and ogled right back. Let him stare. She didn't have to be skinny to type.

Eventually, he stepped back and gestured her into his cavernous foyer. Against her better judgment, she went.

"Elise, you said?"

Ms. Bravo to you, she fervently wished she had the nerve to reply. "Elise. That's right."

"I'm Jed."

"I know."

"Who sent you?"

"My half sister Nell said she thought you might be looking for a new assistant today."

"Nell Bravo, you mean?"

"That's the one."

He frowned, considering. "That was enterprising of Nell."

Elise could easily lose patience with this guy. "Do you need a new assistant or not?"

Was that a smirk on his face? "Fair enough then, Elise." The smirk vanished to be replaced by an expression of utter boredom. And then he said in a tone that commanded and dismissed her simultaneously, "Let's see what you can do."

He really did piss her off—not that that was a bad thing. Her irritation made her determined to show him he'd be an idiot not to hire her. Because Nellie was right. She was a damn fine typist. But more important, she was a Bravo and a Bravo didn't let some big, grouchy butthead intimidate her.

"This way." He turned on his heel and started walking.

She went where he led her, through a fabulous three-story great room, down a hall at the back to a two-story home office with a breathtaking view of the mountains and one entire floor-to-ceiling wall filled with books. The opposite wall was padded, covered in burlap, had a number of bull's-eye targets hanging from it and was scarily studded with what appeared to be stab marks.

Okay, so maybe he played darts. But stab marks? Surely not...

"Sit here." He pulled back the high-end leather desk chair in front of a computer with a screen the size of Cleveland.

Her heart pounding wildly, she sat.

He stood way too close behind her. She swallowed hard and pressed her lips together to keep from ordering him to back off. When he reached over her shoulder, she had to steel herself not to flinch as she felt the heat of his big body.

So close, she could smell him. He smelled really good—like cinnamon. She stared at the ropy tendons in his muscled forearm, at the silky brown hair that dusted his tanned skin, at the sheer size of his big hand as he tapped on the keyboard.

A document popped onto the screen.

He withdrew his hand and backed off, moving over so that he stood in her line of sight. "Start a new paragraph." As the cursor blinked tauntingly at her, he explained, "I'll use your name as the signal to start and stop. When you hear 'Elise,' you will type the next word I say and keep typing every word I utter until I speak your name again. And so on. Are we clear?"

"Crystal."

He made a grunting sound, as though he doubted that. "Do not speak. Not one word." He paused, as if expecting her to say something and thus prove she was incapable of following instructions. *Fat chance, buddy.* When she only waited, he added, "Fake the punctuation. We'll clean it up in edits. Elise."

Did he think she wouldn't be ready? Ha.

He began, "It was a day for killing underlings." She typed each word as it fell from his mouth. "A day without mercy, the sky a gray wolf, crouched on the land, hungry and unforgiving. The man in the watch cap was waiting for him at the station as agreed Elise." He said her name so softly, without even a hint of a pause to signal it was coming.

But she was ready. She punched in a period after the word *agreed* and stopped typing. The room was suddenly totally silent. A strange, hot little shiver raced beneath her skin as she waited, fingers poised on the keyboard, for the sound of her name.

Finally, almost in a whisper, he said, "Not bad, Elise." And they were off and running again. "The man thought he was safe, thought he understood his place and his function. He assumed he would come through this in one piece as long as he did his job. But no one was safe. It was the nature of the game they played. Jack didn't want to kill the man. And maybe, if things went as planned, he wouldn't have to. Too bad things so rarely proceeded as planned…"

Jed went on, his deep voice rising and falling.

Breathing slowly and evenly, Elise had found that calm space she'd learned to inhabit back in Mrs. Clemo's second period keyboarding class. So few people took keyboarding, even back then. But Elise had, because you never knew when it might come in handy to actually be good at something so basic, something most people nowadays just fumbled their way through.

Elise let his words wash into her, through her, and then pushed them out her fingers as he kept on.

And on. Sometimes his voice was eerily soft—and sometimes he shouted.

She tuned out his unnerving changes in volume and tone and stayed with her task, typing the words as he spoke them, throwing in punctuation wherever his pace and phrasing seemed to indicate it, stopping when she heard her name, and then waiting—calm, ready, silent—until he said her name again.

There was something about typing that just worked for her, that was as effortless as drawing her next breath.

Not that she'd ever want to type for a living. Uh-uh. Too much sitting. For the long haul, she needed a job with variety, a job where she didn't have to spend all day on her butt.

But Nellie had mentioned a looming deadline, hadn't she? How long did he have? A few months at the most? Elise could be a typist for three months. If the money was good enough.

About twenty minutes after he started dictating, Jed said her name yet again—and after that, he was silent.

She cast him a quick, questioning glance.

With one big arm across his chest and the other elbow braced on it, he stroked the scruff of beard on his square jaw, a calculating gleam in his eyes. Finally, he spoke. "The typing test is over. Swivel that chair around." She turned her chair to face him. "Can you go on like that for hours?"

She took a minute to consider the question.

It was a minute too long, apparently, because he muttered impatiently, "You may speak now."

"Thank you," she replied with a sarcasm he either didn't notice or chose to ignore. "I would need a five-minute break every two hours, long enough to stand up and walk around a little."

"I can accept that."

"An hour for lunch."

He scowled as he continued to stroke his rocklike jaw. Apparently, in his world, typists shouldn't be allowed to waste precious time on food. But then he conceded, "All right. An hour. But you'll need to be flexible as to *which* hour. If the story's flowing, you might have to wait a while to eat."

"Even with regular five-minute breaks, there have to be limits. No more than five hours at a stretch without an hour-long break."

A grunt of disapproval escaped him. But then he agreed, "Five hours. All right. The work will be intense and you'll need to roll with that. I have to get a book out fast and I'll need you when I need you—which will be ten to twelve hours a day. You will have to live here and you will work six days a week, with Sundays off."

Live here in his house? God, it sounded awful. But in the end, it was all about the money. If the money was good enough, she could bear a whole boatload of awful.

And wait. What about Mr. Wiggles? He would have to come with her. "I have a cat. My cat will be moving in with me."

Dead silence from Walsh. He stopped stroking his jaw and moved to the windows. For several seconds, he stared out at the mountains.

It appeared that Mr. Wiggles was going to be a deal-killer. Well, so be it. She'd barely gotten the big sweetie out alive during the fire. If she had to live with this strange, grumpy man, Wigs was coming with her. Or she wouldn't come at all.

Jed turned those intense eyes on her again. "Fine. Bring the damn cat." She felt equal parts triumphant that she'd won her demand and let down that she was one step closer to being Jed Walsh's typing slave for she still didn't know how long. She was about to ask him how long the job would last when he said flatly, "Unfortunately, I find you sexually attractive. That *could* be a problem." Did he actually just say that? Another of those odd shivers swept through her as he added thoughtfully, "But then there's the cat. I hate cats. That should help." Frowning, he kept those cold eyes steadily on her. "You're thinking I shouldn't have told you that I'm attracted to you. But *I* think it's better if we're on the same page."

She probably shouldn't ask, but she couldn't resist. "What page is that, Jed?"

He didn't miss a beat. "The one where you know that I'm aware of you as a woman, but we both know that work is the focus here and we will be keeping it strictly professional."

Elise said nothing. Really, what was there to say? The less the better, clearly. She shouldn't be flattered. But she was, a little. Apparently the extra pounds she'd put on since the fire didn't look so bad on her, after all.

"My deadline is November first and it will not be extended."

"Four and a half months." She mentally calculated the money that might be hers.

"It's likely you'll be finished by mid-October, but I need you to commit till November first, just in case I run into trouble. I do most of my rewriting while composing the first draft of the manuscript. So essentially, the book is finished when I get to the last page. Then I clean it up, but that I usually can do on my own in a couple of weeks, max."

"All right. Four to four and a half months, then."

"Yes. If you last, the position will become permanent. It's a grind when I'm on a project. But as I said, I type my own rewrites, so as soon as I've made it to the end of the first draft, I probably won't need you until I start the next book. You'll have weeks and sometimes months off at a time between books."

Elise thought of all those thousands he supposedly would pay. She could almost let him think she might be willing to type his novels long-term to get a chance at that money.

But she *wasn't* willing, no way. And it was only right to let him know up front. "I'm sorry, Jed. If we can come to terms, I'll do this one project. But as of November first, I'll be moving on."

His scowl deepened. "I pay well."

"So I've heard."

"If you work out, I'll need you to stay on."

"Sorry, not happening. I'm done the first of November. If you can't accept that, then—"

He cut her off with a grunting sound. "All right. Have it your way. Even if you make it through the trial period, you're done when I finish this book. If it turns out we work well together, I'm not gonna like it, but I need someone ASAP. Let's move on to the money. You'll be an independent contractor. You pay your own insurance and deal with your own taxes."

"Not a problem if the money's right."

"Three thousand a week."

Amazing! When this ordeal was over, she could have enough to get Bravo Catering up and running again. Her heart raced in excitement and her palms started sweating at the prospect. But really, why stop there?

She wiped all signs of greedy glee from her face and manufactured a serene smile. "Four thousand a week."

His cold stare went subzero. She was dead certain they were done here and she knew a moment of stark regret. No, she didn't want to sit in a chair all day typing her fingers to the bone, but she did want that money.

And then at last, wonder of wonders, he nodded. "All right. Four." She was just breaking into her mental happy dance when he added, "*If* you last. We'll start with a three-day trial at five hundred a day."

She opened her mouth to shout out a *yes*. But some contrary creature within her spoke up first. "I'll have my own room, correct?"

He looked down his blade of a nose at her. "Of course."

"Just to be clear, I will need my own bathroom, en suite."

"There are six bedrooms in this house." He was wearing his bored face again. "Each has its own bath."

"I want to see the one where I'll be staying, please."

He asked wearily, "Would you prefer the ground floor or upstairs?"

Choices. She loved those. Lately, there had been so few. "Where is your room?"

Green eyes narrowed. "And that matters, why?"

"I need my space."

He made a humphing sound. "I have half of the upper floor."

"Ground floor, then." She really did need a place to go where he wasn't. "Show me, please."

Jed's expression asked why she insisted on wasting his precious time. But all he said was, "Follow me."

She rose and went after him, back through the great room and down another hallway. He stopped at a door and pushed it inward.

The room on the other side was larger than her apartment over the donut shop. It had a king-size bed and its own sitting area, with a big-screen TV above the modern gas fireplace. The wide windows revealed another beautiful mountain view. There was even a set of French doors leading out to a small private patio. She could hardly wait to settle in.

"Walk-in closet there." He pointed at one of the two interior doors. "I hope this will do," he said, heavy on the irony.

She had one more question. The most important one. "May I see the bathroom?"

"Be my guest." He gestured at that other door.

Elise marched over and pushed it open.

Pure luxury waited on the other side. She'd never been much for the rustic look. But in this case, she could definitely make an exception.

The woodwork was dark and oversize, breathtaking. Travertine tiles in cream and bronze covered the floor and climbed halfway up the walls. The long vanity had two sinks and copper fixtures. There were separate stalls for the toilet and the open shower, which had side jets and a rain showerhead.

Very faintly, she smelled cinnamon. Jed had come to stand behind her in the doorway. "The towel racks have warmers, of course," he said. "And the floor is heated."

"Of course," she said softly, transfixed by the glorious sight of the giant jetted tub tucked into its own windowed alcove. The tub windows had center-mounted cellular shades that could be raised to the top to block glare, or lowered to the bottom for privacy. She could stretch out in bubbly splendor and stare at the sky.

"Well?" Jed demanded.

She turned and met his eyes. "When do you want me to start?"

Chapter Two

Elise Bravo was a find.

Jed knew she was going to last.

He'd known it the minute he'd let her in his house. She wasn't like the never-ending string of hopeless cases he'd hired and fired in the past year. She could type like nobody's business while keeping her mouth shut and not getting frazzled or riled. There was something downright soothing about her, something receptive. She was exactly what he'd been afraid he would never find again. At last.

And he liked looking at her. He could go for her, definitely. She was so soft and pretty, round-faced and bright-eyed, with just enough junk in the trunk. She smelled good, as well. Fresh. Like clean sheets.

She also had attitude. Jed liked a woman with attitude. He liked a woman who could hold her own.

Not that he'd ever make a move on her. Any woman could provide sex. But a skilled assistant was a pearl beyond price. He'd learned that the hard way during the past god-awful year after Anna deserted him.

So yeah, he'd resigned himself to the fact that he wasn't going to be seeing Elise naked. It was going to be all about the work. He'd taken his last extension on this book. With Elise at the keyboard, he would knock the damn thing out.

"I need to get to work immediately," he said.

"I understand. But first I have to get my cat, move my things and settle in a little."

The cat. For a moment, he'd almost succeeded in forgetting the cat. "We'll start tomorrow morning, then," he said grudgingly.

"Yes. All right, tomorrow." She cast a glance over her shoulder at the bathroom behind her, as if to reassure herself that it was actually there. She really seemed to like the bathroom. *Whatever floats your boat, Elise.* She could spend every free moment in there for all he cared. Just as long as she performed during the long working hours. "What about meals?" she asked. "I'll need to have the use of the kitchen while I'm staying here."

"No problem. I have a cook-housekeeper, Deirdre, who comes in five days a week. She'll make plenty for both of us. But if you want to cook, knock yourself out. You can consider the kitchen and any food and drinks you find in it yours."

"Works for me." She looked up at him expectantly. Probably because he was blocking her path. "I should get going…"

He felt a definite reluctance to let her out of his sight. Anything could happen. What if she changed her mind about working for him? Got hit by lightning? Got in an accident bringing over her stuff and her damn cat? He warned, "We start work at zero-eight-three-zero hours sharp."

"That's eight thirty, right?"

"Correct."

"No problem. I'll be here and I'll be ready."

He reconciled himself to letting her go. Turning for the outer door, he doled out necessary info as he led her along the hall to the front of the house. "It's a four-car garage. You can have the bay on the far left. Before you go, I'll get you a garage-door remote, a house key and the code for the alarm system…"

At her apartment, Elise parked in her space by the Dumpster and entered the building through the back door. The hallway and the stairwell smelled of donuts from the donut shop in front. She'd grown to hate that smell, mostly because it tempted her constantly. There was something so perfect about a donut, after all. Flour and fat and sugar, deep-fried and glazed or frosted. The purest sort of comfort to a desperate woman's soul.

Well, bye bye, temptation and hello, jetted tub. So what if she had to type Jed Marsh's book for a living? She'd have a bath every night and make buckets of money. Life was looking up.

Mr. Wiggles was waiting when she opened the door. "Mrow?" he asked.

"Wigs!" She scooped him up, all twenty-plus super-fluffy pounds of him. He was orange, with a huge, thick tail and a deep, loud purr. She buried her face against his lionlike ruff. "We are moving today," she told him.

"We'll keep this dump for now, I think. And reevaluate our crappy living situation once the job is over."

"Mrow, mrow," Wigs replied, as though he understood every word she said. He butted his big head against her cheek to let her know how much he loved her. She gave him one more kiss for good measure and then set him down to start packing.

Her cell rang as she was piling clothes into three suitcases spread open on the lumpy bed.

It was Nellie. "Well?"

"Nailed it."

"You got the job! I knew you would."

"I have to live there, in his house."

"I built that house and Chloe designed the interiors." Chloe was their brother Quinn's wife. "You're gonna love it."

She thought of the bathtub, of the king-size bed. "Oh, yes, I will. And the money is good. Really good."

"That's what I wanted to hear. What about Jed? Seriously, you think you can put up with him?"

"He's not so bad. A little weird. A lot intense."

"Sexy, though, right? In a club-you-senseless-and-drag-you-to-his-cave sort of way."

For some unknown reason, Elise felt a hot flush rush upward over her cheeks. "Don't even go there. He's my boss now and we're keeping it strictly professional."

Nell's naughty laugh echoed in her ear. "You have way more scruples than can possibly be necessary—and we have to celebrate. I'm buying the drinks."

"Rain check. I need to get moved in over there tonight. The job starts early tomorrow morning."

"He gives you crap you can't handle, you call me."

Elise's cheeks were still burning. She could almost

smell cinnamon. And what about that crazy thing he'd said? *Unfortunately, I find you sexually attractive.* "Oh, I think I can handle him."

Nell laughed. "There. That's what I've been missing. You've got your attitude back."

She felt all misty-eyed suddenly. "Thank you, Nellie."

"Hey. What's a sister for?"

"We, um…we're all right now, you and me. Aren't we? I mean, I know I was a total bitch to you back in the day…"

"Back in the day? You and Tracy treated me like crap right up until Clara's almost-wedding to Ryan." That was nearly two years ago now. Clara hadn't married her best friend, Ryan McKellan, but she had somehow succeeded in healing the lifelong breach between Elise and Nell—*and* Nell and Tracy.

Elise defended her absent bestie. "Don't be too hard on Tracy. She always just followed my lead." But not anymore. Tracy was forging her own way now.

Nell laughed again. "You're right. It was all your fault. But I did get my licks in, too. Remember that time I put bubblegum on your breakfast-nook chair?"

Elise started laughing, too. "I loved those yellow shorts. They were never the same."

"It's what you get for messing with me."

"I know. You're so scary."

"Oh, yes, I am. And don't you forget it."

"Never. And I guess what I'm asking is, do you forgive me for all the mean things I did?"

Nell gave a soft sigh. "You know I do."

"I'm so glad."

"Leesie? You're not getting sappy on me, are you?"

Elise swiped at her damp eyes. "No way. Gotta go."

They said goodbye and Elise made quick calls to Clara and Jody, to tell them she had a job typing Jed Walsh's newest book and wouldn't be in at the café or Bloom the next day.

Then she finished packing and dragged her suitcases down to her car, followed by all the cat gear and, last but not least, Mr. Wiggles. He rode in the front seat, sitting up tall beside her, watching the world go by and making those cute little chirping sounds, his own personal brand of kitty conversation. He loved the car and he never got in the way of her driving, so she'd given up on making him ride in his carrier.

She took the space in the garage that Jed had assigned to her and carried Mr. Wiggles in first, pausing in the utility room to check the alarm. As it turned out, Jed hadn't armed it when she left, so she didn't have to mess with it right then. She went on down a hallway and then through the kitchen and great room and down that other hall to her bedroom suite, finding no sign of her employer along the way.

Which was just fine. She had a lot to do and she didn't need the distraction of dealing with her big, crabby boss.

In her room, she put Wigs down in front of the window, promised him she would be right back and went out to start hauling everything in, taking care to shut the door as she left so he wouldn't get out. Jed had said he hated cats. No reason to test his patience right off the bat.

By seven, she had everything put away and her stomach was growling. Wigs, meanwhile, alternately circled his empty food bowl, chased the cleaning robot she'd started up a few minutes before and made a big show of scratching at his three-level activity center.

"Okay, okay. I'm on it." She'd stored his food in the utility room, which had seemed the most logical place for it. She scooped up his food bowls—for wet and for dry—and went out the door again.

The hallways and great room and kitchen were empty. Very odd. Her first night in his house and Jed had vanished into thin air.

She considered peeking into his office, or even looking for him upstairs.

But the thought of wandering through the unfamiliar house trying to track him down made her even more uncomfortable than not having a clue as to where he'd gone. So she went ahead to the utility room to dish up Wigs's dinner. She was pulling the top off a can when she heard music.

She shouldn't snoop.

But really. Where *was* he? And, no, wait… A better question was why did she care?

Well, she cared because…

Okay, fine. She had no idea why she cared.

She set the opened can on the counter and stuck her head out into the hall. Yep. Music.

She followed the faint sound back out into the great room, to the wide central staircase that switched up and back from the lower level to the top floor. It was coming from downstairs, the basement level. She leaned over the railing, listening. It was something with a hard beat, but the sound remained muffled, indistinct. Maybe there was a TV room down there. Her curiosity increased. She left the railing and started down the stairs, catching herself on the second step.

No, she told herself sternly. *Bad idea. Mind your own business*.

So she turned and retraced her steps back to the utility room, where she dished up the food and took it to her hungry cat.

"Mrow?" Wigs left off stalking the cleaning robot to get to work on his dinner.

Now what?

Her stomach growled again. Jed had said that she should make herself at home in the kitchen. She'd grab something to eat and then get up close and intimate with that glorious tub.

It was weird, raiding the refrigerator of the stranger she now worked for—and lived with, essentially. But the food looked good. She heated up a plate of roast chicken, mashed potatoes and mixed veggies and set herself a place at the table that would have looked just right in the castle of a medieval king. She even poured a glass of the pinot grigio she found in the door of the fridge—hey, the bottle was open. Why not? Pulling back one of the big, studded leather chairs, she sat down and smoothed her napkin in her lap.

Definitely weird. Just her, all alone at the massive slab of a table in the giant great room.

She'd just lifted her glass and taken a nice, big gulp of wine when Jed asked from behind her, "You all set up, then?"

Startled, she choked. Wine sprayed out her nose. Coughing and gagging, she shoved back her chair and pressed her napkin to her face. It wasn't pretty. Ragged, hacking sounds alternated with desperate wheezing as she tried to catch her breath.

"Breathe," he commanded. He was at her back by then, pounding on it with his enormous hand, instructing, "Slow, easy. That's the way."

After a terrifying minute or two wherein she wondered if she would ever breathe again, her throat loosened up. She sucked in a decent breath of air at last.

"Okay?" he asked warily.

After wiping the last of the wine from her cheeks,
she turned to faced him—and almost choked all over
again at the sight of him. Shirtless, he had on a pair of
low-riding training shorts that displayed the sculpted
tops of sharply cut V lines. His big, chiseled chest was
dusted with manly hair and dripping sweat. He had a
towel slung around his neck, one end of which he was
using to wipe more sweat from his forehead.

Mystery solved: there was a gym in the basement.
She'd heard his workout music.

Somehow, she managed to croak out accusingly,
"Don't you ever sneak up on me like that again."

For that she got a lifted eyebrow and a disdainful "I
never sneak." And then he asked again, "You okay?"

"Splendid. Thank you."

And just like that, he turned and walked away. She
stared at his broad, sweaty back as he strode to the
staircase. He went up, pausing to look down at her just
before he reached the first landing. "Zero-eight-three-
zero hours tomorrow. Be ready to work."

Like she was some scatterbrained child incapable of
remembering the simplest instructions.

Four thousand a week, she reminded herself. Four thousand and a jetted tub. She nodded, sat back down, picked
up her fork and did not glance toward the stairs again.

The next day was just as Elise had expected it to
be. Endless.

She typed and she typed some more while Jed al-

ternately paced and loomed over her, sometimes shouting loud enough that she winced at the sound, now and
then murmuring so softly she could barely make out the
words. Luckily, she had excellent hearing and managed
to get down every whispered word he said. Already, it
was something of a point of pride for her that she could
keep up with him and never have to speak while at the
keyboard, not even to ask him what he'd just said.

He finished the scene he'd tested her with the day before. Jack McCannon, Jed's ongoing main character—
and, Elise suspected, his alter ego—ended up killing
the man at the station, whose name was Gray. Elise
felt a moment's pity for Gray, whom Jack eliminated
through the clever use of a ballpoint pen to the throat.
Jack, apparently, was quite creative vis-à-vis weaponry.
He killed Gray with a Bic and kept fishing line in his
pocket. Because who knew when he might need to tie
someone up or strangle them with a makeshift garrote?

After Gray met his end, Jack evaded a pursuer and
then met a contact at a café. They drank espresso and
Jack received critical information stored in a minichip
invisible to the naked eye. The contact, Lilias, caressed
his face and transferred the minichip to his cheek. Lilias
was gorgeous. Jack had history with her. Intimate history. Jack considered having sex with her again, but
decided against it due to time constraints and the fact
that he really didn't trust her. The men Lilias slept with
often turned up dead.

There was a scene at a shooting range. Jack was a
crack shot. Who knew, right?

And, yes, already Elise found herself keeping up a
snarky mental commentary on Jed's work-in-progress
as she typed away. The typing really was like breath-

ing. She didn't have to think about it. Even with the
yelling alternating with growls and rumbles, she found
Jed's voice easy to sink into, as if she'd been listening
to him all her life, as though some part of her mind
knew what he would say before he formed the words.
It left her the mental space to have a little fun at Jack
McCannon's expense.

Not that Jed wasn't good at what he did. Now and
then she got so involved she almost stopped typing to
enjoy the story. The action scenes were spectacular—
really edge-of-your-seat.

How many books had Jed written? Four or five, she
thought she'd heard. Maybe she'd have to try the first
one just for the heck of it. It wouldn't hurt to have a little background on the job.

They worked until six thirty that evening. When Jed
finally dismissed her, he stayed behind in the office
to look over the day's pages. She fed Wigs his dinner,
raided the refrigerator and called Tracy in Seattle to
see how she was settling in and report on her new job
with Jed.

Tracy knew her too well. "But you hate typing," she
pointed out. "What is going on? I really don't get this."

"It's amazing money and it's only for four months."

"But what about Bravo Catering?"

As she'd been doing for weeks now whenever she
and Tracy talked, Elise evaded the question. "I'm getting there. This came up, is all. And I thought, for this
much money, why not?"

Tracy wasn't buying. "Just how broke are you? I can
lend you—"

"Trace. Stop. It's tight, but I'm managing."

"I never should have left you."

"Yes, you absolutely should have. It was time and you know it." They'd grown up together, literally. Their mothers had been best friends. She and Tracy had shared the same playpen as babies. Then when Tracy's parents died in a house fire, Tracy had moved in with the Bravos. In every way that counted, Elise and Tracy were sisters, bonded in the deepest way.

They'd gone to CU together and had come home to open their catering business and live in adjoining apartments. But Tracy had always been a science nerd and what she'd never told Elise was that her real dream had nothing to do with planning weddings, designing perfect dinner parties or creating tasty menus that stayed fresh on a steam table. Not until after the fire had Tracy finally confessed that she dreamed of a career in molecular biology.

Well, Tracy was getting her dream now. She'd enrolled in a master's program at the University of Washington.

"I should come home, at least for a few weeks. The semester doesn't start until mid-August."

"Come home for what? Not to see me. I'll be working six days a week, ten hours a day."

"That's insane."

"Yeah, it is, a little. It's also what I want. And I have to tell you, I'm damn good at it, too."

Tracy laughed. "I thought you said this was your first day."

"I have a talent for it. He went through a whole bunch of assistants before I came along. They couldn't handle it. I can."

"What's he like?"

"Jed? Antisocial. Hates cats. Seems to know a lot about deadly weapons."

"He sounds awful."

"I'll say this. He's buff. Looks amazing without his shirt."

"I'm not even going to ask."

"A wise decision."

"You said he hates cats. How's Mr. Wiggles taking that?"

"So far, I've managed to keep the two of them apart."

"Leesie, I just feel bad about deserting you."

"Don't. I mean it. You didn't desert me. I'm doing just fine. Now, tell me what's going on with *you*."

Tracy hesitated, but then she did confess that she'd met a guy she liked. On Friday they were going out to a great Greek restaurant and then to hear some hot Seattle band. She had her fall schedule worked out around the TA and lab-assistant jobs she'd found. She loved Seattle. It was her kind of city.

Elise hung up feeling good about her friend. Yes, she missed her. A lot. But it was about time Tracy came in to her own.

And so far, working with Jed wasn't as bad as she'd thought it would be. She grabbed a sexy paperback and headed for the jetted tub.

Elise was waiting at the keyboard when Jed entered his office at 0830 the next morning. He felt a deep satisfaction just at the sight of her there, in knit pants that hugged her fine butt and curvy legs and a pale blue shirt that clung to her round breasts. They got right to work.

At a little before ten, the cat appeared. The thing was huge. It came and sat in the doorway to the office and watched him with unblinking eyes. Elise had her back to it and had no idea that the creature was there.

Well, fine. Let the cat stare. Jed went right ahead with the scene they were working on.

Eventually, the cat yawned, stretched and wandered off down the hall, its long, hairy tale twitching. Jed waited until they broke for lunch to tell Elise that the animal had gotten out.

She gasped. "Why didn't you say anything?"

"We were working," he replied, though it should have been patently obvious to her.

"But I don't get it. I'm sure I closed my door. How did he get out?"

"Why ask me? You think *I* left your door open?"

For that, he got a snippy little glare. She ran out calling, "Wigs! Come here, baby!"

The damn cat actually answered her. "Mrow? Mrow-mrow?"

He stepped over into the open doorway in time to watch it bound up the hallway to meet her. She scooped it up and buried her face in its hairy belly. "Bad, bad boy," she said in a tone that communicated zero displeasure. Jed felt a stab of actual jealousy. He wished she'd bury her nose in his belly like that. "Come on now," she cooed at the fur ball. "Back to our room…" She slung it over her shoulder and carried it off. The cat, its big hairy paws hanging down her back, watched him smugly through sharp golden eyes, until she turned the corner at the great room and they both disappeared from sight.

The annoying cat aside, that day went even better than the first, Jed thought. He got twelve usable pages by the time they packed it in at 1815 hours. There was just something about Elise Bravo, something soothing and stimulating simultaneously.

The woman was smart. She strictly observed his initial instructions and never spoke while he was writing. With her, as with Anna, he could concentrate fully on the next sentence, on the way the story was coming together.

Plus, every time she got up to stretch, he got to watch. He could write poems to her backside. And those breasts. He would love to get his hands on them. There was something about her, the softness of her, that he wanted to sink into, the way she bit the inside left corner of her mouth when he picked up the pace and the words were flying, her fingers dancing so fast over the keys.

He liked to move in close and suck in that clean-sheet scent of hers. And he got a kick out of the way she talked to him, sharp and snippy, but somehow with patience, too.

Elise did it for him in a big way. She wasn't beautiful. She was so much better than beautiful. She was… the exact definition of what a quality woman should be.

No, nothing was going to happen between them. They both understood that.

But that didn't stop him from enjoying the view, whether she was sitting, stretching or walking away. And he saw no reason he shouldn't take pleasure in imagining the lusty things he was never going to do to her.

The next day, the final day of her trial period, he introduced the knives.

Chapter Three

Jed found his knives both soothing and stimulating. In that sense, they reminded him of Elise. For him, there were few experiences as calming as a well-thrown knife. He often threw them while he worked. The knives were an integral part of his process. They increased his focus. He liked to send them sailing. And he liked the sound they made when they hit the padded wall that Bravo Construction had installed precisely to his specifications.

He'd put off introducing the knives to Elise. He dreaded the possibility that she might freak—or worse, walk out and not come back. And there he would be again, with no assistant, his deadline looming.

Not being all that nice of a guy, he'd often used the knives to get rid of typists who weren't working out. No, not by stabbing them, but by simply hurling a sleek *kunai* or a combat bowie knife without warning. More than one unsatisfactory keyboarder had screamed good and loud when surprised in that way.

But he wanted to keep Elise, so he prepped her.

When she entered the office for work that day, he was waiting for her, an assortment of knives laid out on the credenza next to the door.

She said, "Deirdre is here. She says good morning."

He grunted. Deirdre Keller was a perfectly acceptable cook and housekeeper. Beyond that, he had nothing to say to her. He certainly didn't require her to tell him "good morning."

And Elise had spotted the knives. She caught on immediately. "Okay, I get it now. The padded wall, right?"

Feeling strangely sheepish, he confessed, "I like to throw while I'm working. It clears my mind."

She glanced at the array of knives, then at the wall in question. "What about all the targets? Do you throw darts, too?"

"Just knives." She seemed puzzled. So he elaborated, "I throw the knives at the targets sometimes. And sometimes I just send them flying at the wall. It depends."

"On…?"

He hadn't expected all these questions. But he was willing to indulge her if answering her would keep her happy. "I honestly don't know what it depends on, why sometimes I want to hit a target and sometimes I just want to throw—the scene I'm writing, I guess. Or the mood I'm in."

"Have you ever missed the wall and hit your assistant?"

"Not once." He couldn't resist adding, "Though now and then, I've been tempted."

A burst of laughter escaped her. He found the happy sound way too charming.

"Oh, you're just so scary, Jed."

"Yes, I am," he replied darkly. "And you should re-member that." She had that look, as though she was purposely *not* rolling her eyes. He added, "And as you can see, your desk is over there." He gestured in that direction. "And the wall is there." He indicated the wall. "You won't be in the path of a throw unless you get up and put yourself between me and the wall."

"What about if you get tempted?"

"I won't." *Not to throw a knife at you, anyway.*

"Hmm," she said, as though still suspecting she might end up a target one of these days. And then she asked, "Is this it, then?"

"Define *it*."

"Will there be more potentially life-threatening ac-tivities you're going to want to do while I'm in this room with you?"

He admitted, "Sometimes I clean my firearms. Handguns. Machine guns. Assault rifles. That kind of thing. I find cleaning weapons—"

"Let me guess. Soothing."

"Yes. Exactly."

Those fine dark eyes gleamed. "You find the strang-est things soothing."

He almost allowed his gaze to stray downward to her breasts. "You have no idea."

"I'm going to assume that when you clean your guns, you make sure they aren't loaded first."

"You assume correctly."

Her gaze narrowed. "Anything else you find sooth-ing while you work? Archery, maybe?"

"I haven't used a bow and arrow in years, but it's a thought."

"So I should be prepared for that?"

"No. Knife throwing is my impalement art of choice."

She hummed again, low in her throat. "That's a real thing? Impalement art?"

"It's usually referred to in the plural. Impalement *arts*. Strictly defined, impalement arts entail throwing dangerously sharp objects at a human target."

She considered. He loved to watch her think. "Like at the circus."

"That's right. A circus knife-thrower is in the impalement arts. A circus archer, too. Hatchet- and spear-throwers, as well." She reached out and brushed her fingers over the stacked leather washer handle of a full-size USMC KA-BAR straight edge. "That's the most famous fixed blade knife in the world," he said. "It was first used by our troops in World War Two."

She slanted him a glance. He couldn't tell if he'd amused her or she found the knives fascinating, or what. For a moment, neither of them spoke. He wasn't big on extended eye contact as a rule. But he didn't mind it so much with her.

She broke the connection first, her gaze sliding away.

He shook himself. "You ready, then?"

By way of an answer, she went to her desk and fired up the computer.

Jed threw a lot of knives that day. And he wrote a lot of pages. It was good. Really good. Elise took his knives in stride. She never turned a hair when he sent one flying. She just kept right on filling those blank screen pages with his words.

They worked until 1900, at which point he handed her a check for 2,832 dollars and told her she was officially hired.

She frowned at the check. "I thought we said fifteen hundred for the first three days."

"I included payment for tomorrow and Saturday at your full rate. And after this week, I'll pay you every Saturday at the end of the day."

She rose. "Works for me." She headed for the door to the hallway.

He caught himself with his mouth open, on the verge of calling her back and asking her to have dinner with him.

Not a good idea. She had her life. He had his. They met each morning for work and went their separate ways when the workday was through. He found her far too attractive to start sharing meals with her.

Fantasies involving her were fine—or rather, given that he was having them, he might as well roll with it. Fighting it too hard would only make him want her more.

But hanging around with her after hours?

Bad idea.

She lived in his house. It would be so easy to get more than professional. That would be stupid. Because when the heat between them burned out, the work would get strained. She would end up leaving.

And that couldn't happen.

He was keeping her. She just didn't know it yet. She thought she was quitting when this book was through. But she was wrong.

Before she had knocked on his door Monday, he'd been increasingly sure that his big-deal writing career was headed straight for the crapper. He'd spent way too many sleepless nights sweating bullets over his dawn-

ing realization that Anna had been a lucky fluke and
he would never find the right assistant again. Now that
he *had* found her, he would simply have to convince
her to stay. So what if she seemed determined to go?

One way or another, whatever he had to offer her to
keep her happy, he *was* keeping her.

And the best way to lose her was if they had a thing
and then it ended—which it would. He'd never been
any good at relationships. Sooner or later, most women
wanted more than he knew how to give. Maybe Elise
was different. Maybe she could have a good time and
then have it be over and still sit down at the computer
and type his words for him every day.

But he couldn't afford to take a chance on finding
out.

So he kept his damn mouth shut as she disappeared
down the hall.

As they'd agreed when he hired her, Elise had Sunday off.

That Sunday, she left the house at 0905 hours. Jed
knew the time exactly because he was standing on the
balcony outside the master suite when she backed her
car out of the garage.

Unlike the previous Monday, when she took off to get
her cat and her clothes, he was okay with watching her
go. Today, he felt zero anxiety as she drove away. They
were getting on well together, after all, and he was paying her an arm and a leg. No reason she wouldn't return.

Plus, he hadn't seen the cat in the car. And if the cat
was still here, she would have to come back.

An hour later, he headed for the shooting range,
where he remained until lunchtime. He had a burger at

a truck stop out on the state highway and got back to the house at 1400 hours.

Elise was still gone.

He put on workout gear and went down to the basement to use the StairMaster and then pump iron for a couple of hours. After his workout, he had a shower and found something to eat in the fridge. Then he went to his office and researched poisons until past 1900 hours. He had a lot of book left to write and that meant a lot of characters to kill.

Elise still hadn't returned.

He wasn't concerned. No reason to be. As long as she showed up at her desk on time in the morning, he couldn't care less where she went or how long she stayed there.

But for some completely crazy reason, he was kind of worried about the damn cat. Had she taken the animal with her, after all? Or had she just left the poor thing alone in her room?

Yeah, he hated cats. But she shouldn't just leave it locked up like that all day. Wasn't that cat abuse?

Sure seemed like it to him.

An hour after he left his office, he wandered down the hallway that led to her room. He stood there in front of her door for several minutes and debated the acceptability of trying the handle, maybe letting the fur ball out—if it was in there and if she'd left the door unlocked.

But opening her door without her permission seemed like a really bad idea. She might get mad if he did that. And getting her mad was no way to keep her working for him.

In the end, he settled on putting his ear to her door, just to listen for the possibility of plaintive meowing.

"What are you doing, Jed?"

Luckily he had nerves of steel. He didn't so much as flinch at the sound of her voice—even though he felt like a bad child caught with his grubby hand in the candy box.

Slowly, he pulled his ear away from her door and stood to his full height, turning to face her as he did it.

She watched him from the far end of the hallway, a stack of boxes in her arms. "Well?"

The best defense is always an offense. "Your damn cat. I was getting worried about it." He strode toward her. "Here. Let me help you with those."

She allowed him to take the boxes. "But you hate cats."

"Open the door."

She eased around him and did just that. It wasn't locked.

The cat was there waiting. It didn't look any the worse for wear. "Mrow? Mrow-mrow?"

"Wigs!" She scooped it up, scratched its big head and kissed it on its whiskered cheek. "How's my big sweetie?"

"Mrow-mrow." It started purring, the sound very deep. Rumbly. Like an outboard motor heard from across a misty lake.

Elise said…to Jed this time, "Just set those down inside the door. Thanks."

He set the boxes where she wanted them and then turned to leave, figuring he'd escape before she asked him any more questions about why she'd come home to find him with his ear pressed to her door.

No such luck. "Why where you worried about Wigs?"

Resigned, he stopped and faced her again. "You left the cat locked in there all day. That can't be good."

"Well, that's kind of sweet of you." She seemed bemused.

He hastened to disabuse her. "I am never sweet."

She actually giggled. He despised gigglers—or at least, he always had until this moment. She held up the cat. It hung from her hands, totally relaxed, and big enough that its rear paws dangled at the height of her knees. "See? He's fine. I left him plenty of food and water. He doesn't mind a little alone time."

"A little? You've been gone for eleven hours."

Her soft mouth pursed up. "It's my day off. How is it any of your business how long I've been gone?"

It wasn't and they both knew it, which meant there was absolutely no point in answering her. So he didn't.

Eventually, she got tired of waiting for him to defend himself and informed him icily, "I have one day off a week and I had a lot to do."

Yeah, he felt like a jackass. But somehow, he couldn't just apologize for invading her private space and move on. "That's a big cat."

Her mouth got tighter. "Thank you, Captain Obvious."

He narrowed his eyes and flattened his lips. "That cat needs space."

"He's fine in my room. My apartment is a studio, smaller than my room here. He was perfectly happy there."

Smaller than her room here? That was way too small. And she was a Bravo. He'd grown up in the area and he knew of her family. The Bravos had always had enough money to be comfortable, at least. The Bravos didn't live in cramped one-room apartments. He wanted to ask her how she'd ended up in one.

But that would be a personal question and they were

not getting personal. "Next time leave your door open, that's all I'm saying."

She blinked as that statement sank in. "You mean, let Wigs have the run of the house?"

Suddenly, his throat had a tickle in it. What was that about? He never got a ticklish throat. He coughed impatiently into his hand. "Yeah. And come to think of it, don't lock that cat up in there at all. Let it have the house to roam in."

A tiny gasp escaped her. "You mean, all the time?"

"Isn't that what I just said?"

"But what about how you hate cats?"

"I'm making an exception in this case," he growled at her. She looked at him with distinctly dewy eyes, so he commanded, "Don't make a big deal out of it."

"I…well, okay. I won't."

"Good," he said, scowling as hard as he could. And then he turned on his heel again and started walking away fast.

"Jed?"

He stopped. But he didn't turn. "What?" he grumbled at the great room in front of him.

"Thanks."

He almost said *You're welcome*, but caught himself just in time.

In the next week, the work continued to go well. Very well. Elise just kept typing, never dropping a word or making a sound, no matter how loud and aggressive he became while acting out the voices of his characters.

On Thursday, he cleaned three of his rifles and a couple of Glocks as they worked. She seemed to take that in stride—didn't even bother to comment when she saw the weapons, gun oil, cleaning rags and brushes laid out that morning on a folding worktable.

Jed had never been a happy man. He found the concept of happiness more than a little silly. A man did what he had to do in life and what he had to do was rarely that much fun.

But with Elise working out so well, the pressure was off in terms of his deadline and hopefully his career. He was getting more work done, faster, than when he had Anna. It was a hell of a relief. Maybe this was happiness.

If it was, it wasn't half bad.

The damn cat had free rein of the house. The animal talked too much and had a tendency to climb up on tall cabinets and drape its giant body on the wide-beam staircase railings and along the backs of couches. But so what?

Jed had told Elise that the cat could roam free and he wasn't a man who reneged on his word. He ignored the creature. It wasn't that hard.

Another week went by, as smooth and productive as the previous one. Jed dared to feel confident that he was out of the woods at last. He was going to make it. He would have the book turned in by the final deadline— or maybe even before, at the rate they were going. Elise was a damn treasure.

His only concern now was her plan to leave once this project was finished. He really needed to do something to keep that from happening.

Fortunately, he had until November 1 to figure out what.

Two and a half weeks after he hired Elise, Jed woke at 0200 to a rumbling sound.

He'd been dreaming of a misty lake and the soft roar

of a motorboat coming toward him through the fog. Shaking off sleep, he pulled himself to a sitting position and peered blearily into the darkness.

Gold eyes gleamed at him from down by his feet and the strange rumbling sound continued. The motorboat had followed him right out of his dream.

But it wasn't a motorboat.

It was the damn cat.

"Out!" he commanded, sweeping an arm toward the door for good measure.

But the cat was not impressed. It just watched him and continued to purr.

He stared it down for several seconds and then ordered, "Get!" good and loud.

No effect whatsoever. In time with the purring, it kneaded his comforter with its big paws.

Jed gave up glaring and growling and took action. Shoving back the covers, he scooped up the animal into his arms. Unconcerned, the cat kept purring as Jed carried it to the upper hallway, set it on the floor and firmly shut the door on it.

The next morning, he purposely went down to the kitchen early, when he knew Elise would be there.

And she was. He found her at the counter near the six-burner range with eggs, butter, a golden loaf of home-made bread, milk and several spices spread out in front of her.

The staircase met the ground floor just beyond the open-plan kitchen. She glanced over her shoulder and spotted him as he descended the last few steps. That wide mouth bloomed in a smile of greeting.

Strange. It was only a smile, yet it caused a distinct and disorienting stab of pleasure right to his chest.

"Jed. What a surprise." She turned to face him fully. She looked good, fresh and well rested in curve-hugging jeans and a big, white shirt of some silky material that clung to her tasty breasts.

He kept the corners of his mouth turned down and spoke with great severity. "I need a word."

Her smile vanished. He missed it the second it was gone and regretted being the reason it went away.

What was she doing to him? He wasn't sure he wanted to know. He entered the kitchen area. Her dark brown eyes were wary now. "Of course," she said. "Coffee?"

Why not? He grabbed a mug and poured himself a cup. She waited for him to say what was on his mind, her breakfast preparations suspended. "Your cat was in my room last night. I woke up and found the thing purring on the end of my bed."

"I'm sorry."

"Don't be sorry. Get control of it."

"No problem. I'll go back to keeping him in my room."

"No." He turned to lean against the counter. "I didn't ask you to lock the thing up. I just want you to keep it out of my room when I'm sleeping. I like leaving my door open at night, but I don't like waking up to a giant purring cat on my bed."

"I understand. I'll take care of it."

"Fair enough, then." He started for the stairs.

He'd taken a single step when she offered, "Care to join me? I'm making French toast."

Something good happened in his chest right then, a warm feeling. Kind of...cozy.

He did want to join her, he realized.

He really did.

But he *should* refuse her. Sharing meals was getting too friendly, stepping over the line.

But then again, maybe he was going about this all wrong. Maybe he didn't need to stay away from her to keep her.

Maybe he needed to get closer—no, not in a man-woman way. He had sense enough to see that getting into a sexual relationship with her was too risky in the long run.

But what about buddying up to her? That should be safer. And if they were friends, he'd have a better chance of convincing her to stay.

Then again, buddying up? Who was he kidding? He wasn't one of those guys that women made friends with. He got that, knew that he would never win any prizes in the personality department.

But she seemed a social sort of creature. If she had to be alone with him in his house day after day, shouldn't he put a little effort into making the experience a positive one for her?

"Stay," she said again, and she did seem to mean it. "Let me give you a delicious breakfast to make up for Mr. Wiggles messing with your sleep."

She was being nice to him. Come to think of it, she'd been nice to him often lately. Because of the cat? Probably. After that first Sunday, when he'd told her she should let the cat free in the house, she'd seemed to loosen up around him.

He'd come to like it when she was nice to him. He wouldn't mind if she was nice to him all the time.

"With bacon?" he asked hopefully.

And she smiled at him again. "Bacon, too. Absolutely."

"Well, then, yeah. I'll take you up on that."

So he set the table for both of them. He poured himself more coffee and settled into his chair as the wonderful smells of frying bacon and sweet spices filled the air.

When the food was ready, she brought him his plate, the silky sleeve of her white shirt brushing his shoulder as she set down the meal in front of him. He felt the slight pressure of her arm beneath the fabric. It was nothing, an accidental touch.

But it didn't feel like nothing. To him, that touch was a thunderbolt straight to the heart—and lower down, too. All at once, he was acutely aware that he hadn't been with a woman in almost a year.

He reacted on instinct, grabbing her wrist as she put down the plate. "What are you doing?" The words rumbled up from the depths of him.

"I… Nothing." Her wrist bones felt fragile in his grip, the skin over them far too soft. "Really, Jed. Not a thing." She was shaking a little.

Was he scaring her? He hadn't meant to scare her. "Don't brush up against me." He released her. "It's not a good idea."

Her stomach was flip-flopping and her mouth had gone dry, so Elise straightened and stepped back from him.

What had just happened?

Oh, please. She knew what had happened.

She'd gotten too close and he wanted to scare her off. Because he'd really meant what he said that first day. He was attracted to her and he didn't want to be. She shouldn't let that please her so much.

But it did.

She set down her own plate, pulled back her chair

and sat. Smoothing her napkin on her lap, she hid a
sly smile and remembered the way he'd looked at her
when he came downstairs this morning, a burning sort
of look, a look that could almost have her imagining
that he found her irresistible—which was totally crazy.
She was so not the irresistible type. Men never gave her
burning looks. They looked at her fondly or indulgently
or sometimes like maybe they wished she would quit
talking, but never as though she might be driving them
wild with desire.

Just the possibility that she might have that kind of
effect on Jed gave her a lovely little thrill. Because Jed
was…well, if a woman could go for the strong, scary,
noncommunicative type, he was hot. Way hot. And
lately, in the past week or so, as she soaked in her bub-
ble bath at night or caught a glimpse of him on the way
upstairs, bare-chested and sweaty after a workout, she
found herself thinking that she *could* get interested.

Not that she would. Uh-uh. That would be seriously
unprofessional. Not to mention, hadn't she made enough
bad life decisions in the past few years? She finally had
a job that could put her back on track. No way would she
mess up this chance by falling into bed with the boss.

Jed let out a groan.

She slid him a glance. He had his eyes closed and
he was chewing slowly. Pure pleasure showed on his
hard face.

Her French toast?

Sure looked like it.

She hid another smile. Her French toast was quite
excellent if she did say so herself.

He swallowed. "Damn it to hell. On top of everything else, you cook."

Did those rough words make her feel lovely and desirable and talented? Oh, yes they did. Talk about a boost to her battered ego. Impossible macho madman Jed Walsh saw her as capable and sexy and maybe even slightly irreplaceable. He was a tough critic, yet he found her exceptional—at work, in the kitchen and as a woman.

She hadn't realized how much she needed that, how much she yearned for a little admiration, for some honest appreciation.

After all those endless months and months of doubt and fear and awfulness, Jed's reluctant approval was a vindication. As he groaned over her French toast, Elise felt strong. Indestructible. A superheroine.

But only for a moment. The surge of powerful emotion was just too much. She was the queen of the world—and then her fragile equilibrium snapped.

Hot tears welled, pushing at the back of her throat. Her cheeks burned and her heart set up a wild, out-of-rhythm tattoo. In the space of an instant, she hurt so much and she hated herself for it.

Just a moment of confidence. A flash of womanly power.

And she was completely undone.

She had to get out of there before Jed saw her like this and knew she was not the unflappable super-assistant he believed her to be.

Shoving back the heavy studded chair, she tossed her napkin on the table.

Jed looked up, startled, a slice of crispy bacon halfway to his open mouth. "Elise? What's the matter?"

Clapping her fingers over her mouth to hold back the sobs, she whirled and raced for the sanctuary of her room.

Chapter Four

Bewildered, Jed called after her, "What the hell, Elise?" But she was already gone.

As she vanished into the hallway that led to her room, Jed set down the slice of bacon without taking a bite of it. What had just happened? He could have sworn those were tears he'd seen in her eyes.

Tears? Elise?

Not possible. She was far too tough for tears.

"Mrow-mrow?" The fur ball trotted toward him across the great room.

"Not a clue," he answered, as though the cat had actually asked him a question.

Was he losing it?

Quite possibly.

The cat bounded to him, plopped down at his feet and stared up at him expectantly. "Mrow?"

"Yeah." He stood and tossed his napkin onto his chair. "You're right. We'd better go check on her." He headed for the hallway to her room, Mr. Wiggles in his wake.

When he got to her door, he tapped on it gently. "Elise?"

"Go away!" she shouted from the other side.

Going away was exactly what he wanted to do, but somehow he couldn't. What if she was sick and needed a doctor? What if she did something crazy in whatever strange state she was in?

He tried the door handle. Locked. "Elise, come on. Let me in."

"I said, go away!" She shouted it even louder that time. And then she sobbed—a short sound, swiftly muffled. But definitely a sob, no doubt about it.

"She's crying," he whispered uneasily to the cat. It returned his gaze steadily, but had nothing helpful to offer.

Jed decided to try coaxing, though God knew he was no good at that. "Elise." He tried to make his voice gentle. "Come on, now. Let me in…"

"Go away, Jed!"

He probably *should* go. She'd made it more than clear that she didn't want him there.

But that seemed plain wrong, somehow. He had decided to try and be her friend, hadn't he? Well, clearly, she needed a friend right now and he was the only one available—well, except for the cat. And what could a cat do at a time like this?

Carrie had always said he was hopeless when it came to understanding what went on in a woman's head and heart. He knew his ex-wife was right. What could he do to help right now?

Most likely nothing.

"I give up," he said glumly to the cat.

He turned and started back up the hall—at which point he heard the click of the lock disengaging behind him. Relieved and yet simultaneously terrified of the hundred ways he could screw this up, he turned back to the door as it slowly swung inward.

She looked so small. He hated that. The Elise he knew might not be all that tall, but she carried herself proudly, head back, shoulders straight.

She wasn't proud now. She hung her head and her shoulders sagged. And she was sniffling, her pretty eyes red and her nose even redder.

It hurt him to see her this way. "Aw, now. It can't be that bad."

"It can, Jed. It is." And with that, her face contorted and she burst into tears again.

This time, she didn't even try to hide them. She just stood there, clutching the door handle, her pretty face twisted, tears running down her cheeks. That was the worst, to see her so broken, to see her drooping and sobbing, stripped of her pride.

What should he do? He had no idea. But it turned out not to matter. His arms just kind of reached for her without conscious direction from his brain.

That was all she needed. With a hard sob, she threw herself against him. What could he do but gather her close?

"There now, there." He patted her back, feeling awkward. Inadequate. But she wasn't complaining. She scrunched in even closer, crying hard enough now that he felt the dampness of her tears through his shirt. "It's okay, it'll be okay," he promised, though he had nothing on which to base that assumption. "Come on. Sit down." He guided her into her room and over to the sitting area, where he pulled her down onto the sofa with him. Alternately patting her back and smoothing her hair, he held her and waited until she ran out of tears.

Eventually, she sniffled and asked, "Tissues?" into the soggy fabric of his shirt. Still curved tight against him she reached out a hand and groped for the box on the coffee table. He gave it to her.

"Thank you," she whimpered on a watery sob, pulling free of his hold and scooting away from him. Huddled against the sofa arm, she began whipping out tissues, dabbing at her wet cheeks and blowing her nose. Once she'd mopped up most of the tears, she let her hands fall to her lap and groaned, "God, I'm a mess."

"No," he lied.

"Yeah." She nodded glumly. "Yeah, I am." There was a long, heavy sigh. She tossed the wad of tissues toward the wastebasket in the corner and tugged at her shirt, straightening and smoothing as she squared her drooping shoulders.

The cat, which had jumped up and stretched out on the back of the couch during her meltdown, lifted its giant orange head from its paws and asked, "Mrow?"

"Fine, really," she replied. Then she looked directly at Jed for the first time since he'd pulled her into his arms. "Well." She tried for a brisk tone and mostly succeeded. "We should get to work, huh?"

He thought of his page goal for the day. Screw it. "What made you cry?"

A soggy little snort escaped her. She patted at her hair. "Believe me, my list of reasons is endless and you don't need to hear any of them."

"Sometimes it helps to talk about it." Did he actually just say that? Never in his life had he willingly offered to listen to a woman tell him her problems. But this was different. This was Elise, who kept her cool no matter how many knives he threw, who typed his words steadily, error-free and unflaggingly, two hours at a stretch, ten to twelve hours a day. Elise, who was simultaneously soothing and stimulating. And because it was Elise, he really wanted to know.

Elise studied his craggy face. Those jade eyes regarded her, unwavering.

She should ask him to leave now, say she would meet him in the office in fifteen minutes. And once he was gone, she should wash her face and comb her hair and get ready to work.

It had to be a bad idea to confide in a man whom everyone in town thought was crazy, a guy who cleaned his guns while he killed off bad guys and good guys alike, one by one. A guy who signed her paychecks, for crying out loud.

But, oh, he'd been wonderful just now. Gentle and caring and patient while she sobbed uncontrollably and dripped tears all down the front of his T-shirt. He'd been a complete sweetheart and she was so tired of holding her head up, of remembering her pride, of keeping it all inside.

For once, she would just like to tell *someone* all the things that had gone wrong in her life.

"You'll be sorry," she warned.

"Tell me," he said.

So she did. She told him about her trust fund that had matured when she was twenty-one, of the thousands of dollars she'd thrown away in the stock market because she'd been so sure she could figure out for herself which stocks were the best bets. About the bad boyfriend, Sean, a struggling artist who'd coaxed twenty thousand from her a year and a half before, supposedly as an investment in the Denver art gallery he was opening with several "world-famous" artist colleagues. As it turned out, there was no gallery and those colleagues didn't exist. Sean vanished with her money never to be seen or heard from again.

And Biff Townley, who'd been her friend forever. Biff's wife was a cheater who walked out on him and then took him to the cleaners in the divorce. Biff had only needed a little help, he said, to get back on his feet financially. Elise had lent him the money he needed so badly. Then he'd declared bankruptcy. "He said he was so sorry, but he couldn't pay me back my money because he'd been forced to discharge all his debts and he needed to start over with a clean slate."

And then there was the fire. "It took everything, including all our catering equipment. There was insurance money, of course, but my debts and bills had been piling up. I'd spent a whole bunch on renovating my apartment and I was paying it off in installments—small installments as the money got tighter, so I still owed a lot on that. I couldn't put off paying anymore. And my best friend, Tracy, was half owner of the building and the business. After the fire she finally admitted to me that she'd never really wanted to be a caterer, that her dream was to move to Seattle and study biology. That was the worst."

He frowned. "Which?"

"Tracy moving away." Her throat clutched. "That was the hardest blow of all."

"Elise?"

"Hmm?"

"Are you going to cry some more?" He looked kind of worried.

"You know, I just might—and aren't you sorry now you volunteered to listen to all this?"

He stuck out his hand. She watched his big, blunt fingers come toward her. He wrapped them around her arm. It felt really good, his touch, so warm and steady and more exciting than she would ever have admitted to anyone.

"Come here," he said roughly. She went where he pulled her, though she probably shouldn't have. He lifted her and turned her so she was leaning back against the rock-solid wall of his broad chest. Then he rested his chin on the crown of her head. "Continue."

Wigs, still stretched out along the sofa back, had started purring. She reached up and ran her palm along the warm, furry length of him.

"About your friend Tracy moving to Seattle…" Jed's deep voice rumbled in her ear.

She petted Wigs and leaned against Jed and realized she felt truly comforted for the first time in so long—comforted by Jed Walsh, of all people. "Tracy and I grew up together. She was the one person in the world I could tell anything to. She never judged me, though the awful truth is that I had some seriously bitchy years."

"What is a bitchy year?"

"Let's just say I wasn't always the nicest person in the world."

"But you are now?" He had the nerve to sound amused.

She would have elbowed him in his six-pack if only the angle had been right. "I still have attitude, I'll admit." He made a low sound. It just might have been a chuckle. She smiled to herself and continued, "But I used to be pretty certain that I knew everything. I was popular in high school."

"You mean all the boys were after you?"

"Hardly. I mean I was kind of bossy."

"Not possible."

"I'm going to pretend you meant that sincerely."

"Good idea. Continue."

She tried to think of something quelling to say to him. Nothing came, so she went on with her story. "I had a certain way of taking command of any given situation. I also treated some people like crap, like they were beneath me. I would snub them, you know? And say rude things behind their backs, even start rumors about them. So maybe it wasn't such a bad thing that I had it all and then threw it away. Maybe losing everything kind of showed me that I had a lot to learn."

He was silent, but his arms held her just a little tighter.

She forged on. "Anyway, Tracy was always the one person I could tell all my troubles to. But now she's gone. Now I can't just call her and unburden my heavy heart. If I did that, Tracy would only feel guilty and insist on coming home."

He rubbed his chin, very lightly, across the crown of her head. "Do you want her to come home?"

Her heart still cried yes. But she did know better now. "Tracy needed to go. It was time for us to find our own separate lives. So the answer is no. I want her to have what *she* wants, what she needs. I want that most of all."

"I asked you what *you* want, Elise. Do you want your friend to come back home?"

She drew a slow, shaky breath. "No. I don't think we *could* go back now, anyway. I think we're set on new paths and it wouldn't work to try to be what we were before."

That day, they had lunch together. Over sandwiches and chips, they talked about the scene he'd been working on when they broke to eat. She told him she thought Jack had too easily turned the tables on a mysterious woman with a scorpion tattoo who'd come after him with a syringe full of potassium chloride. Jed took the criticism well, she thought. And then he really surprised her by reworking the scene when they went back to the office, drawing out the tension before the scorpion lady got a deadly dose of her own medicine.

And that evening, he showed up when she was in the kitchen dishing up her dinner. He loaded up a plate for himself and they sat down together.

The next day was Saturday. He didn't eat with her at breakfast or lunch, but he showed up at dinnertime. They talked about it—about how they both kind of liked having meals together—but neither of them wanted to be locked into meeting up every time they ate.

So they agreed: no mealtime expectations. They spent so much time in the same space as it was, it would be easy to get sick and tired of each other.

But Elise wasn't getting sick and tired of Jed. Far from it. Every day she grew to like him more. She liked the way he listened to her, with such steady, serious attention, as though determined to absorb every word. And the way he treated Wigs—with a heavy dose of irony and grudging respect. He was kinder than he wanted anyone to know.

And goodness, he looked amazing without a shirt. He really got her lady parts humming. She could get interested in him in a big way.

But she wouldn't. They'd forged an excellent working relationship and that was nothing to fool around with. Sex would only mess with the program and she couldn't afford that. She was getting out of this with the nest egg she needed.

However, it couldn't hurt to know more about him. She would like to consider herself a friend of his. And she'd been meaning to read the McCannon books in order. It might give her insight into what made him tick. And it couldn't hurt on the job, to have more information about the stories that had preceded the current one.

There were five of them so far, she found out when she looked them up online. And all of them were available in audiobook. She downloaded the complete set for her iPhone so she could listen in the bathtub.

That Sunday, her sisters took her to the Sylvan Inn for lunch. The inn, on the highway a few miles from town, had excellent food and a homey, cozy atmosphere.

Elise joined not only Clara, Jody and Nell, but also Chloe, who had married their brother Quinn. Their cousin Rory McKellan came, too. And so did Ava Malloy, a Realtor who represented Bravo Construction whenever one of their houses went up for sale.

It was the first time they'd all been together since Elise started working for Jed. Sunday wasn't the best choice for a girls-only get-together, but it was the only day Elise had now and her sisters had put aside various family commitments to make it happen.

They sat down and ordered and then they all wanted to know how it was going with Jed.

"You've lasted how long with him now?" Nell sounded thoroughly pleased with the situation.

"On Tuesday, it will be three weeks," Elise replied with considerable pride. She raised her glass of white wine. "To you, Nellie. I can't thank you enough for finding me this job."

Nell laughed. "I love it when you're grateful." They all lifted their glasses and shared in the toast.

"I don't believe it." Ava, petite and adorable with long blond hair, looked pretty close to awestruck. "The way I heard it, nobody could last with that guy."

"He's not so bad." Elise set down her glass and reached for a fluffy, hot dinner roll.

"It's a triumph," Nell declared. "I knew you would be the one to tame that wild beast."

"I wouldn't call him tamed, exactly. But we get along."

Rory said, "I heard he was raised in the woods, just him and his reclusive survivalist father, that his mother died when he was really young." Elise had heard that, too. Most people in town knew the basic facts about the famous Jed Walsh.

Clara made a sympathetic sound. "That must have been hard for him."

Ava said, "And he was military, right? And married for a while."

"What's he like to work for, really?" Jody asked.

"Kind of scary at first." Elise described how he acted out the scenes. "He also throws knives while he's working."

Jody scoffed, "You're kidding, right?"

"Believe it." Nellie backed up Elise. "We built him a special padded wall to throw the knives at."

"He cleans weapons, too," Elise added. "It's part of his *process*, he says. And he demands absolute silence from me while he's dictating."

Chloe said, "It sounds awful."

"It took some getting used to. But believe me, the money is excellent and I find that very motivating. Plus, I guess I'm kind of getting used to Jed."

Jody was watching her a little too closely. "Ohmigod. You like him. I mean, you *really* like him..."

There were giggles and grins as Elise tried not to blush. "I told you. I've gotten used to him. And he's been kind to me, that's all."

"Kind, how?" demanded Nell.

Elise sipped more wine. "Long story. Not going into it today."

Nell gave her a too-knowing look. "Jody's right. You could go for him."

"But I won't," Elise replied with a lot more confidence than she felt.

Monday morning, Jed came into the kitchen as she was getting the oatmeal going. She offered to share and he accepted.

When they sat down to eat, she asked him, "So who typed your books before I came along?"

Was that almost a smile on his way-too-sensual lips? Sure looked like one. "Didn't you hear? I've had an endless chain of typist-assistants. I terrorize them and then they disappear, never to be heard from again—which reminds me, never enter the walk-in closet in my room."

"I see. It's where you keep the bodies, isn't it?"

"Just call me Bluebeard." He made a show of stroking the beard scruff on his chin.

But she wasn't letting it go that easily. "You've written five *New York Times* bestsellers. The last three made it to number one."

"Been reading my book jackets, haven't you?" He stirred brown sugar into his bowl.

She added raisins to hers. "Come on. You followed me to my room the other day and helped me through my meltdown. I'm grateful, Jed. And I would really like to know you just a little better."

He took a very slow, very careful sip of coffee. And then he shrugged. "Her name was Anna Stockard." He said the woman's name too quietly. Was he sad? Regretful? With Jed, it was difficult to tell.

But Elise thought she understood. "You were in love with her."

"Hardly." He was wearing that sardonic expression of his—the one that passed for amusement.

"What? That's funny?"

"Anna was calm. An excellent typist, like you. Unlike you, she was also a motherly woman in her fifties." *Motherly.* And his own mother had died when he was very small. "She typed my first book for me, which I started not that long after I left the service."

"Had you written before?"

"Fiction? Never."

"What made you decide to write a novel?"

He looked at her so patiently. "So. We digress?"

"You're right. I shouldn't have interrupted. I do want to know about Anna."

"But you also want to know what made some guy

raised in a one-room cabin by a half-crazy doomsday prepper imagine he could write bestselling thrillers."

"I wouldn't have put it exactly that way," she said gently.

"I know." He spoke as softly as she had. "My father was not only a paranoid survivalist who homeschooled me and taught me most of what I know about knives and firearms and living off the land, he was also a reader. He read everything he could get his hands on. He built a shed next to our cabin just to store the books, which he scrounged for free, showing up at the end of garage and estate sales when the sellers just wanted to get rid of what was left. He read to me. A lot. Those are my best memories growing up—him reading to me and later, as his eyesight failed, me reading to him. We got through all the great books of the western world, my father and me, before he died. And he loved a good thriller."

"Well. Now your brilliant career as the creator of Jack McCannon makes perfect sense. What did your dad die of?"

"A fall. He had cataracts and they just got worse and he hated doctors, so he never had the surgery that would have saved his sight. He fell from the front steps of our cabin and hit his head on a rock."

"I'm so sorry."

"Why do people always say that?"

"I don't know—because we feel sympathy and we don't know what else to say, I suppose. How old were you when he died?"

"Eighteen. I went straight into the service."

"And Anna? How did you meet her?"

"Anna was a widow. She rented the other half of the North Hollywood duplex I owned with my then-wife,

Carrie. I was in my late twenties by then. Anna was a great cook." *Like you.* He didn't say it, but she could see it in his eyes. "And Anna was lonely, I think. She was always dropping in with casseroles and cupcakes to share. I told her about the book I was trying to write and how I thought I needed to hire a typist, how I'd figured out that sitting at a computer didn't work for me. I needed to be up, moving around, saying the words out loud."

"So Anna volunteered?"

"That's right. Turned out she'd been a legal secretary for years. I hired her. And she was terrific. Carrie and I broke up when that first book, *McCannon's Way*, sold for seven figures at auction. Carrie got half the advance and her ticket out of a marriage that wasn't working."

Elise wanted to know what had happened with Carrie, but she was afraid he might clam up if she asked. Then again, he seemed relaxed, willing to tell her about his life. If he didn't want to get into it, he could just say so. "What went wrong there, with your wife?"

He made a low, amused sound. "I was wondering when you would get around to asking me that."

"You don't want to talk about it?"

"I'm fine with talking about it." He ate a spoonful of oatmeal. "I met Carrie when I was stationed in San Diego. We were kids, really. Both of us just twenty-one. I decided I was in love with her the first time I took her to bed. I proposed. She said yes. We got married and moved in together. And then we grew out of each other—or maybe we just slowly came to realize that we never had that much in common in the first place. And we never spent all that much time together, anyway. I kept re-upping, partly because I felt useful serving my country and partly because I didn't know what I would do with myself once I was a civilian again. Carrie got tired of waiting for me to come home. But she stuck. And then I finally left the service. I was home all the time and we had to face the fact that whatever we might have had once, it was gone. Divorce was the right thing for both of us."

"But Anna stayed with you when your marriage ended."

"Yeah. I bought a great house overlooking the ocean on the Oregon coast and Anna moved there with me. She worked with me through books two, three, four and five. She not only typed, she cooked meals and ran the house. It was all going so well."

"And then...?"

"Anna had two grandchildren in Phoenix and her daughter was going through a tough divorce. A year ago, Anna decided to move in with her daughter and take care of the kids. Exit Anna. Enter a bad case of writer's block. I started hiring typists. You know the rest. None of them worked out, not until you."

"What brought you back to Justice Creek?"

"After three months or so of getting nowhere on the book, I got this brilliant idea that going back to my roots would help me focus. It didn't." He was staring off toward the large oil painting of weathered barn doors on the wall opposite his seat at the table. But then he turned that green gaze on her. A shiver went through her, a lovely, warm one. He said, "What helped me focus was Anna. And now what helps me focus is you."

Jed felt good. Really good, for the first time in over a year. The book filled his mind. He had scenes all lined up, ready to be written.

He felt so good, he was even nice to his agent, Holly Prescott, when she called just as he and Elise were getting down to work.

"I need to take this," he said to Elise. "Fifteen minutes?"

"Good enough." She left him alone, pulling the door shut behind her.

He put his agent on speakerphone and dropped into Elise's chair. "What can I do for you, Holly?"

"Jed. You sound great."

"Thanks. And I'm working. What?"

"I have a surprise for you. We're in the process of getting you a spot on *NY at Night*. You'll hear from the publicist to set up the details for the trip."

The last thing he needed right now was to fly to New York to be on some talk show. "'In the process.' What does that mean?"

"It means it's going to happen and it will be sometime next month, though we're not confirmed on the date yet. I just wanted to tell you ahead. I knew you'd be pleased."

"Are *you* pleased, Holly?"

"Very."

"Then speak for yourself. I, personally, am on a deadline. You know about deadlines. They have to be met in order for books to get published."

"Jed, don't be a douche bag. It's *NY at Night*."

"So get me a slot in November—or better yet, during the next book tour."

"You know it doesn't work that way with a popular show. You've got to take it when they're willing to have you on. And next month Drew is running a whole series with top authors." Drew was Andrew Golden, the show's near-legendary host. "And can't you please be a *little* excited? Come on, Jed. *NY at Night*."

"You keep saying that as though I'm suddenly going to have a different reaction."

"Once we get the date, the publicist will call with all the details."

"I don't have time for this."

"But you will *make* time—and the book?" she asked, switching subjects so fast he was lucky he didn't get conversational whiplash. "Going well?"

"It won't be if I have to break my rhythm to fly halfway across the country just to kiss some talk show host's ass."

"But it *is* going well?"

"I'm afraid to admit it to you," he grumbled. "You might put me on another talk show."

"I am really glad to hear this," Holly said fervently. He got that. She'd been just as worried as he was that his case of writer's block might never end.

He gave in and confessed, "Yeah, I'm relieved, too."

"You finally found an assistant." It wasn't a question. Holly understood his process. She'd been representing him from the first.

He thought of Elise and felt good about everything. "Yes, I did. Her name is Elise Bravo. She's just what I needed."

"Pay her a lot and never let her go."

The good feeling became less so. He didn't like being reminded that he still hadn't figured out exactly how he would convince Elise to stay. "Anything else, Holly?"

"As a matter of fact, yes. Carl's been worried about you." Carl Burgess was his editor and deserved to know that things were going well now.

He promised to call Carl and reassure him. There was more. Jed had turned down two film deals. A third had languished in "development." The option on that one had just expired. Holly had another film offer she wanted him to consider. And there were new foreign-rights contracts she was overnighting to him. Next, she started nagging him about social media. He had a brilliant virtual assistant who handled all that, but Holly wanted him to be more directly involved.

"I'm a recluse, Holly. It's what I do. My readers get that even if you don't."

"But if you'd only—"

"Work, Holly. I need to get down to it."

Finally, she let him go. He called his editor as promised. Carl picked up. They talked for maybe five minutes, Jed promising the other man that he was on top of it now and there would be no more deadline extensions. Then Carl had a meeting. He rang off.

Elise returned a couple of minutes later. The sight of her, so curvy and lush, in white jeans with rolled cuffs and a pretty pink shirt, her dark hair loose on her shoulders, had him realizing that even if his excellent agent drove him crazy and he hated making reassurance calls to his editor, it was a beautiful day.

She asked, "Ready to go?"

He got up from her chair and she took his place.

That day, he wrote double his page goal.

And that night, he had trouble sleeping. But for a good reason. The book filled his head. And when he finally did drop off to sleep, he dreamed plot points, tweaks for rough spots and clever ways to fit in boring exposition.

At some point, a motorboat started rumbling. He was dreaming of the misty lake again.

The cat.

He opened his eyes to find the fur ball curled up right beside him, making biscuits on the comforter, that motorboat purr vibrating against his thigh.

Elise must have left her door open again.

The golden eyes opened. The cat stared at Jed with a blissed-out expression.

It was kind of pleasant, to be truthful—the warmth of the animal against his leg, the rhythmic kneading, the soft, incessant purr. And Jed was still groggy, still half asleep. He had zero desire to get up from the comfort of his bed to put the creature out.

So fine. Let the damn thing stay. He punched at his pillow and settled back into sleep.

The cat was gone when he woke in the morning. He decided against mentioning the animal's nighttime visit to Elise. Let the cat roam free. If it ended up on his bed, so be it. Jed would simply roll over and pretend it wasn't there.

During the hour-long break for lunch, which Elise spent at the kitchen island chatting with Deirdre as the housekeeper prepared their dinner, Jed went downstairs for a quick session on the elliptical. When he came out of the gym into the open area at the base of the stairs, he saw the cat.

The animal sat staring out the French doors that led to a flagstone patio. Jed went over there and opened the doors for it. The cat glanced up at him as though puzzled.

"Well, go on then," Jed said. Mr. Wiggles went out. Jed shut the doors and ran upstairs to grab a quick shower before returning to work.

He didn't give the cat another thought until dinnertime, when Elise seemed preoccupied. They dished up the food and sat down, all without a single word from her. He was about to ask her what she had on her mind when she glanced up from her untouched dinner with a worried frown and asked, "Have you seen Wigs?"

"Not since lunchtime." He said it with a shrug. Inside, however, he felt a definite stirring of alarm. It had suddenly occurred to him that not once in the weeks she'd been living in his house had he seen her let the cat out.

Maybe he shouldn't have done that.

Elise set down her fork. "I keep trying to tell myself he's just fallen asleep in a closet or something and he'll be popping up out of nowhere any minute. But he didn't come when I called him to eat. That never happens."

He stood. "Hold on." He headed for the stairs.

"Jed? What in the...? Where are you going?"

"Be right back," he called over his shoulder as he started down.

On the lower floor, he went straight to the French doors, hoping to find the cat waiting on the other side of them.

No cat. Except for the fire pit and an empty circle of Adirondack chairs waiting in the fading light of early evening, the patio was empty.

If anything had happened to that fur ball, Elise would never forgive him. How would he keep her then?

This was bad.

Plus, well, not that he would ever admit to such silliness, but he'd started to grow rather fond of the creature. So beyond the possible loss of Elise, he would really feel like crap if Mr. Wiggles met an untimely end.

He pushed the doors open and went out. Mr. Wiggles was not anywhere on the patio. He made a quick tour of the area near the house. Nothing.

So he set off at a jog to circle the building.

He called, "Mr. Wiggles? Where are you?" as he went, feeling ridiculous and guilty and increasingly aware that he'd made a serious mistake.

The cat failed to appear.

When he returned to the French doors, Elise was standing on the other side of them. Her big, sad eyes stayed locked with his as he entered. He couldn't bear her looking at him that way, so he turned around and shut the doors. He took a long time about it, far longer than necessary.

But eventually, he had to face her again.

And when he did, she asked the question he'd been dreading. "What's going on, Jed?"

Chapter Five

Bleak acceptance settled over him.

He couldn't put off the inevitable any longer. So he set about the grim task of confessing what he'd done. "At lunchtime, I saw the cat sitting right here, staring out the doors. I figured it wanted to go out."

Except for two bright red spots of color cresting her cheeks, her face went dead white. "You let Wigs out." She spoke at barely a whisper, but the accusation seemed to echo through the lower floor like a shout.

"Elise, I'm so sorry. I'm sure it's around. It'll be back."

"He's an indoor cat. He's never been outside, not once since I adopted him from the shelter when he was this big." She illustrated how small, holding her shaking hands just inches apart.

"Elise, really, I—"

"No. Stop." Her voice trembled like the rest of her. "I

don't even want to hear your excuses. I just don't. You saw him at a door, so you just…let him out? Who does that? Who in the wide world is that freaking oblivious?"

He felt he had to say something, so he muttered, "It's not an excuse. It's more of an explanation."

"Whatever you want to call it, I don't want to hear it."

"But I—"

"Uh-uh. No." Those big eyes glittered with tears. "I told you I lost everything and Wigs is all that's left. And it is *dangerous* out there." She threw out an arm in the direction of the patio. "Bears. Coyotes. Bobcats. Wolves. Who knows what all? Something could hurt him, something could *eat* him. If I never see him again, I don't know what I'll do."

Was she going to lose it right there in front of him? It certainly seemed so. "Elise. Please. I know you're upset, but there's no need to exaggerate."

She gritted her pretty teeth at him and let out an actual growl. "Oh, there damn well is a need. Anything could happen to him. Anything at all."

"Elise. Settle down. Nothing is going to happen to that cat."

She threw back her head and howled at the ceiling, after which she started peppering him with questions, each one louder and more hysterical than the last. "What is the matter with you? What were you thinking? What could possibly have been going through your mind?"

He strove for calmness. One of them had to. "I made a mistake, okay? A big one, apparently. But getting yourself all worked up isn't going to help us find your cat. You need to slow down, take a deep breath and—"

She cut him off with a wordless shout of fury and then commanded, "Get out of my way!" Dodging around him, she threw open the French doors and ran outside. "Wigs! Wigs, come here, baby. Wigs, here kitty, kitty…" She headed for the trees that rimmed the property and called in a high, plaintive voice, "Wigs, here kitty, come on, baby…"

"Elise, hold up…" He took off after her.

She ignored him and kept on going into the trees.

He didn't know whether to follow her into the woods or not. Hesitating by an outcropping of decorative rock, he tried to decide on his next move. She clearly wanted nothing to do with his sorry ass at the moment. He got that, loud and clear.

But given her emotional state, it seemed unwise to let her wander off alone.

So he started moving again, trailing along behind her as she searched the wooded area behind the house, calling for the cat as she went. After about fifteen minutes of that, she led him into a clearing, a small meadow of tall grass and wildflowers. Past the meadow, twin trails wound upward into the trees.

In the middle of that clearing, she stopped at last. Jed halted several yards away and waited to see what she might do next.

But she only let her head drop back. For a good sixty seconds, she just stood there, staring up at the slowly darkening sky. And then, just as he was trying to figure out what his next move should be, she crumpled to a sitting position on a boulder that stuck up through the long grass.

He hesitated to approach. His nearness might just set her off again.

But then she braced her elbow on her knee, plunked her chin on her fist and looked straight at him across the clearing. "It's okay, Jed." She sounded sane again. But how long would the sanity last? "I'm not going to kill you." He didn't find those words all that reassuring, but he started for her anyway as she added drily, "Though I probably should." He kept coming until he stood looking down at her. She tipped her face up to him.

When he offered his hand, she took it. Her slim, smooth fingers disappeared in his grip. He pulled her up and wrapped his arms around her, figuring the chances were about fifty-fifty that she'd shove him away.

But she didn't. With a sad little sigh, she rested her dark head against his chest. "I guess I kind of lost it."

He had to actively resist the need to stroke her silky hair. "It's understandable. You love the damn cat and I really screwed up." She felt good in his arms—too good and he knew it. Too soft, too sweet. He lowered his head and breathed in the scent of her.

She looked up at him then, eyes so bright, both scared and hopeful. "Tell me that he's going to be all right."

He tried not to stare at that wide mouth of hers, not to think about swooping down for a kiss, about how good it would feel if her lips parted, welcoming him. "He'll show up soon. He's going to be fine."

She gave him a slow, irresistible smile. "I think I'm having a moment."

"Why is that?"

"You just called Wigs a *he* instead of an *it*."

He admitted, "Yeah, Wigs and I are working things out. He showed up in my room again last night."

"Did he wake you?"

Jed nodded. "But then I realized he wasn't really bothering me, so I just went back to sleep."

"If he'll only come back, I promise to be more careful about letting him out of my room at night."

"*When* he comes back," he amended her gently.

"Right." Another shaky sigh escaped her. *"When."*

"And as I said, he doesn't bother me. Leave your door open anytime you want to." If he stared at her upturned mouth for one second longer, he was going to taste it. "Come on." He took her hand again and stepped back to a slightly safer distance. "Let's go."

She let him lead her across the meadow and into the trees. The walk back to the house didn't take long at all. When they reached the patio, she wanted to have a look out in front, too.

He said, "I checked there when I first went downstairs."

She turned those shining eyes on him. "Let's just look one more time."

So they circled around the house and walked up and down the winding paths in the steep front yard. They checked the far side of the garage and also the shed farther out. The cat was nowhere to be found.

He kept the front door locked and he hadn't stopped to grab a key on the way out, so they returned the way they'd come, to the French doors off the lower floor at the rear of the house.

Jed spotted the big orange cat when they rounded the corner to the backyard. Mr. Wiggles sat in front of the doors, staring straight at them. He appeared to be fine—alert, calm and uninjured. The relief Jed felt at the sight of the animal was a very fine thing.

"Look." Elise's soft voice vibrated with pure joy.

"Don't run at him," Jed warned quietly. "If he races off, we might lose him again."

"You're right. I'll go slow." She started forward at an easy pace. Jed fell in behind her. "Wigs," she chided in a soft, coaxing tone. "There you are. Where have you been?"

The cat replied with the usual "Mrow? Mrow-mrow."

Jed made out the small gray lump at Mr. Wiggles's feet about the same time Elise did. She asked the cat, "Baby, what's that you've got?"

"Mrow-mrow." Mr. Wiggles bent his leonine head and scooped up the object in question. About then, Jed saw the dangling pink tale.

Mr. Wiggles had brought home a mouse.

Elise gasped as she realized that her sweet baby boy had a dead rodent in his mouth.

Behind her, Jed warned softly in what she'd come to think of as his black ops voice, "Do not start screaming. The mouse is a gift."

She paused long enough to shoot him a dirty look over her shoulder. "Not all women start shrieking at the sight of a mouse."

"Unfair assumption. My bad." She knew he was trying to sound contrite. He just wasn't all that good at it.

And Wigs was what mattered. She focused back on him, moving steadily forward. When she stopped about a foot from him, he lowered the mouse to the flagstones again and then sat up tall. "Mrow."

"Say thank you," Jed instructed. It was actually kind of cute, him trying to school her on the psyche of her own cat.

"I'm on it." She reached down and scooped Wigs up into her yearning arms. "Thank you so much," she whispered, burying her nose in his thick fur, breathing in the unaccustomed smells of pine and dust on him. "I'm so grateful for that dead mouse. And I'm so, so glad you're home."

"Mrow." He'd started purring, the sound growing louder, making a pleasurable vibration against her chest.

She cuddled him closer. "You want your dinner, don't you?"

"Mrow, mrow-mrow." He definitely did.

She turned to Jed and asked, "Would you take care of my...gift?"

"Happy to." He actually smiled, a rarity for him. In the fading light, his eyes were the deepest, truest green. She watched them crinkle at the corners and thought that he was a good man. And also that she'd never been happier than she was right at this moment, with Wigs in her arms—and Jed at her side. "Go on in," he said.

Reluctantly, she broke the hold of his gaze and took Wigs inside.

Jed disposed of the mouse, washed his hands in the utility room and then returned to the table.

The food had gone cold. He grabbed a beer and waited for Elise, who was still off somewhere enjoying her reunion with the cat. Yeah, he could have just zapped his plate in the microwave and dug in.

But he enjoyed having her there with him while he ate, especially in the evenings. It kind of rounded out the day, the two of them together at the dining room table. It was something he looked forward to, something he'd quickly gotten accustomed to, something he fully expected to continue through the completion of his current book.

And every book after that.

She came toward him across the great room, her expression serene. "What are you staring at?"

"You." He thought of the feel of her in his arms, the scent of her that he would know anywhere—and it hit him like the proverbial bolt from the blue.

He was going about this all wrong. Staying away from her in order to keep her made no sense at all.

He needed to get even closer than friendship.

Closer. Dear God. He would love that.

Too bad he was no good at all that love and romance crap. He communicated through his books. Dealing with actual people had never been his strong suit. He'd been a rotten husband to Carrie, spending most of their marriage on a never-ending tour of duty, and not knowing what to say to her, exactly, on the rare occasions when he was home on leave. So far, he was zero and one in the forever department.

And if he went for it with Elise and it blew up in his face, where would he be then? Zero and two—*and* minus the assistant who made it all hang together.

Losing Anna had just about finished him.

Still, the differences between Elise and Anna needed considering. Elise was a woman of his own age, a woman he found desirable. Whereas Anna...

He had cared for Anna, absolutely. They'd been friends—remained friends, to this day. Anna had been good to him. She'd taken excellent care of him. But now, looking back on it, he saw that Anna was bound to leave, bound to go to her daughter and grandchildren eventually.

Family. It mattered. Even though he had no family left, Jed got that most people placed a high priority on having one.

If he managed to keep Elise in a business-only capacity, someday she would want a husband and children to call her own. As far as the books getting done, a husband and children didn't have to be a problem. Elise would meet some local guy, get married, have babies—and continue to make a boatload of money typing Jed's books.

Except Jed didn't even want to think about Elise with some nice, regular guy who would take good care of her and give her babies to love.

"Jed." She'd reached the table and now stood over him, watching him, her smile indulgent, her eyes so bright. "What's going on in that big brain of yours?"

"Not a thing."

"Liar. You've got your scary face on—give me your plate. I'll warm it up."

He handed it over. She took both plates to the kitchen area. He watched her walk away. Always a pleasure, watching Elise walk away.

She set the plates on the counter, got the vented plastic dome from the cupboard, covered one plate, heated it, covered the other and warmed it up, too. "How's your beer?" she asked, when she set his plate back in front of him.

"I'm good." What would it be like, him and Elise, living together, working together, sleeping in the same bed night after night? He was starting to think he really needed to find out. "So the fur ball's all right?"

She smoothed her napkin on her lap. "No thanks to you, Wigs is perfectly fine."

Jed enjoyed a bite of crab cake. "You know that he had a great time outside, right? He got to run free, hunt, bring home the bacon to the mistress he adores…"

"That was not bacon. That was a poor, dead little

mouse and I don't want to talk about it at the dinner table."

"But you can see that it wouldn't be such a bad idea to let Mr. Wiggles out now and then."

She set down her fork sharply. "Do not even *think* it. He's an indoor cat and he's staying that way. You should read the statistics. Outside cats get in fights and get injured. They eat diseased meat. They're targets for parasites and predators. Indoor cats live years longer than cats that are allowed outside." Her eyes flashed with heat and those telltale bright spots of pink stained her soft cheeks. He was tempted to say something else to provoke her, just because he liked to see her spitting fire.

But on the other hand, he didn't really want her pissed off at him. Especially not now that he was re-thinking his own hard-and-fast rule against seducing his secretary. So he picked up his beer and saluted her with it. "I bow to your greater knowledge on this subject."

Her fire turned to sweetness. "Please never let him out again." Her wide mouth trembled. Her eyes held his.

Damn. She really did it for him. He'd been an idiot to try to tell himself he wouldn't end up in bed with her. "I won't let him out again. You have my word on that."

The next day during their lunch break, Jed found Mr. Wiggles waiting by the ground-floor French doors again. The cat stared out at the patio and the rim of trees beyond the yard with an expression that seemed to Jed to be very close to yearning. When a finch flitted down and pecked at the gravel between the flagstones, Mr. Wiggles made chirping, eager sounds. His whiskers quivered in anticipation of the hunt.

"Sorry, big guy. No can do." Jed turned for the stairs and didn't look back, though it did bother him that the fur ball had hunted his first, last and only mouse. All creatures deserved access to the great outdoors.

It wasn't until that night, when he woke to the sound of Mr. Wiggles's motorboat purr and opened his eyes to find the cat lying on the pillow next to him, that he knew what he had to do.

Jed spent a few hours Sunday researching the project. Monday, while Elise was taking her lunch break, he called Bravo Construction.

Nell Bravo was there and willing to take his call. For the past four months or so, he only ever dealt with Nell when he needed something from the builder. It was easier that way. She was smart, tough and direct and never accused him of hurting her feelings. In the past, he'd been brusque with the receptionist and yelled too loud at one of their carpenters. After that, Nell told him he was to deal with her and only her.

Nell didn't say hello. She opened with "You'd better be treating my sister right."

"She's still here. I think you can take that as a very good sign." He realized he needed to make nice. For giving him Elise, Nell deserved a thank-you. "Elise is just what I was looking for. Thanks for steering her my way."

"You're welcome, Jed. And what can I do for you today?"

"I have a project I need built. It's not exactly what you do. But I thought if you couldn't help me, you could refer me to someone who can."

"Happy to. Tell me what you need."

He described what he wanted and then elaborated

a little. "I was thinking a basic structure at first, with maybe add-ons, climbing runs, bump-outs, things like that later, after we see how it works out. I want it to look good, to fit with the landscaping and the house. High-end, you know?"

"I understand. But I didn't have a clue you had a cat."

"Of course I don't have a cat. Do I look like a man who would have a cat?"

"So it's for Wigs, then?"

"Why? Is that somehow a problem?"

"No. I'm surprised, that's all. This isn't exactly your style."

"You mean, because I'm such a hard-ass, I can't do something nice for Elise and her cat?"

"Pretty much. Tell me, Jed." He knew from her tone that he wouldn't like what came next. And he didn't. "Are you a secret softy?"

He had no idea what to say to that, so he demanded curtly, "Can you make it happen, or refer me to someone who can?"

"No way I'm referring you," she said with a low laugh.

"What the hell?" he growled. "Somehow, this is funny?"

"Well, yeah, it kind of is." He was just about to tell her thanks for nothing and hang up, when she asked, "So what time are you through yelling and throwing knives today?"

"When am I done *writing*, you mean? We knock off around nineteen hundred hours."

"Seven works for me. I'll draw up something basic and you can give me more details tonight to flesh it out."

"So you're telling you're going to build it for me and you'll be here at nineteen hundred hours?"

"Yes, I am."

"Excellent." He was relieved. Bravo Construction always did great work. They came in on time and gave him what he asked for, only better. Plus, if had to deal with other people, he preferred people he already knew, people who weren't the least bit afraid of him. The scared ones just never worked out. "When can you start on it?"

"Let me check the schedule before I commit, but I'm pretty sure once you approve the design we can get going within the week."

"The sooner the better."

She made a low, amused little sound. "I might even give you a special discount, being as how it's for Wigs and all."

"Money is no object. I want it to look good, like everything you build. And I want it roomy with lots of climbing, scratching and hiding options. Also, I want it as soon as possible."

"Of course you do, Jed. And at Bravo Construction, we make it our business to see that you get exactly what you want."

He wasn't sure he liked her tone. "You know, Nell. Sometimes I find your attitude humorous."

"How 'bout now?"

He wasn't touching that. "See you tonight. Join us for dinner?"

"Sure, thanks."

"Good, then." He hung up before she could give him more grief.

Besides the money and the jetted tub and the way she was getting to like her grouchy employer way more than she should, Elise appreciated being allowed to dress for comfort while working for Jed. If she had to spend the whole day sitting on her butt, at least she didn't have to do it in a pencil skirt.

Jed said he didn't mind what she wore as long as her clothes didn't constrain her or break her concentration in any way. So she wore leggings and roomy casual shirts. Now and then in the past couple of weeks as the summer turned hot, she even wore shorts. Jed didn't complain about the shorts.

On the contrary, she would often catch him looking at her bare legs with great interest, his eyes kind of glazing over. She loved that. Sometimes when she was typing and couldn't actually see him staring, she knew exactly what he was doing anyway, because he would pause in the middle of a sentence…and then catch himself with a throat-clearing sound. Then he would murmur, "Elise," so that she would stop typing, and follow it with a string of muttered swear words, at which point he would grumble out her name again and lurch back into the story.

That day, she'd started off in leggings and a lightweight tunic. But it was gorgeous out, and hot. At lunch, she'd changed to cutoffs, cowboy boots and a soft plaid shirt, and had taken her sandwich out on the deck off the great room to enjoy the sunshine.

When Jed joined her in the office after the break and she swung her chair around to greet him, he did a double take at the sight of her bare legs—and then instantly tried to pretend that he hadn't. She totally loved that.

He said, "Your sister Nell is coming tonight." He sounded furious. But she was on to him big-time. He often seemed angry when he was flustered. "She'll eat with us."

And wait a minute. Had she heard him right? Jed didn't make a habit of inviting her family members for dinner—he didn't make a habit of inviting *anyone* for dinner. "Okay. I'm just going to ask it. Why is my sister suddenly coming to dinner?"

"I invited her." He had on his scary face.

She rose from her chair. "That thunderous expression you're wearing? Doesn't faze me in the least. And let me put it this way. I'm not typing a word until you tell me what's going on."

He grabbed a bowie knife from the array on the credenza and whipped it toward the padded wall. It landed with a *thwack*. "Don't piss me off. It messes up my aim. You could get seriously hurt."

She sat on the edge of her desk, crossed her legs and thought how handsome he was when he tried to be intimidating. All testosterone and hunky grumpiness. "Are you trying to scare me? Because it's not really working."

He threw another knife. "You Bravo women. You're all about the attitude."

"You're saying Nell gave you attitude?" His answer to that was to send another knife flying at the wall. "I'm guessing that's a yes. What's going on, Jed?"

He had ninja stars, too. He picked one up and sent it spinning. Bull's-eye. Finally, he turned to her. "I wanted it to be a surprise. But then I knew you wouldn't like it if your sister just showed up out of nowhere. And I didn't want to spring it on you in front of her—just in case you don't take it well, you know?"

For a man who used words for a living, he was making a real hash of explaining himself now. "Take what well?"

Instead of answering her question, he scowled and added, "But I can't see why you wouldn't. It's a good thing and you should love it. I know the damn cat will."

"Jed. What in the world are you talking about?"

He picked up another knife and then set it down without throwing it. "Let's go for a walk."

This was a first. "But it's work time."

"Work can wait."

That was so totally not Jed that her mouth fell open. "Are you feeling all right?"

He held out his hand to her. "Get over here."

"You know you need to work."

"Fine. Grab a steno pad and a pencil."

"What for?"

"If I have an idea while we're walking, you can jot it down."

"But—"

"No buts. Think of it as working. Steno pad. Pencil."

She bent over the side of the desk, pulled open the pencil drawer and found both. "Fine." She waved the pad at him. "Got 'em."

"Good. Now, come here."

She got up from the desk. "You're the boss."

"And don't you forget it." He wiggled his big fingers at her impatiently.

She took her time strolling over there, partly because she loved baiting him. And partly to revel in how hard he was trying not to glance down at her legs. When she slipped her free hand in his, she gave him her sweetest smile. "Well, all right. I have to admit that a walk sounds really nice."

Downstairs, Wigs was sitting at the French doors staring longingly at the patio and the woods beyond, the way he'd been doing too often since last Wednesday when Jed had let him out.

"Sorry, sweetie. No can do." She scooped up the cat and set him safely out of the way.

They slipped through the doors and Jed shut them. Wigs stepped up to the other side and sat down to stare out again. He meowed at her, but softly enough that she couldn't hear him through the insulated glass. She got the message, though, loud and clear. He longed for the freedom of the great outdoors.

"Poor guy." Jed claimed her hand again.

She almost yanked it back. "No thanks to you."

"Come on." He said it gently, coaxingly even.

"What is going on with you?"

"Just walk." Pulling her with him, he set off across the patio and into the trees, where the shade made the air a little cooler.

They walked in silence to the meadow and across it. He took the winding trail on the left and they started upward into the forest again. Overhead, somewhere beyond the green canopy of the tall firs, she heard a hawk cry. Small creatures scrabbled in the underbrush. Elise breathed in the warm, pine-scented air and told herself to enjoy the moment.

A stroll in the woods with Jed. Who knew that was ever going to happen?

When the ground leveled out again and the trees opened up to a small, grassy space, he stopped suddenly and turned to her. She gazed up at him, admiring him though she probably shouldn't. His dark hair showed glints of bronze in the sunlight. And he had a little gray at the temples. It looked good on him.

"Might as well get on with it," he said bleakly.

She was all for that. "Great. Talk to me."

"It's like this. *I* want your damn cat to be able to go outside. Your damn *cat* wants to be able to go outside. But *you* want him safe. So I came up with a solution. It's called a 'catio'—get it? Cat patio. Which is too cute by half if you ask me. I want to enclose the back patio in wire fencing and rig one of the French doors with a cat door. Nell will build it for me, which is why she's coming over tonight, to agree on the plans and collect a deposit."

Elise stared up at him, into those green eyes she'd once seen as icy. This man.

Oh, God. This man.

Her arms ached to grab him close and hold him tight and never, ever let him go.

Except that grabbing him would be so stupid. She needed this job, needed to stick with it right through to the end of this book, as planned. She needed every penny he was paying her; she couldn't afford to take a chance on messing it all up. And falling into bed with the boss could definitely mess it all up.

Jed's mouth had a grim twist to it now. "You don't like it. You hate it."

She thought of last Wednesday, of Wigs and that poor, dead mouse. Of Jed warning her not to start screaming. *The mouse is a gift,* he'd said. At the time, she'd been offended that he assumed she would freak, but the point was, a gift mattered. A gift ought to be properly appreciated.

And this man had given her no end of gifts—not the least of which included a big boost to her self-image and self-confidence after the endless series of emotional and financial blows she'd sustained in recent months.

Yeah, there were plenty of reasons to say no to his catio plan. It would cost more than she ought to let Jed spend on *her* pet. And when this job ended, he'd just have to tear it down, wouldn't he? And how would Wigs react, to have a roomy outdoor space to roam in and then end up returning to the confinement of her dinky apartment over the donut shop?

It wasn't fair to Jed. It could be harder for Wigs in the end.

But wait just a second here. Why go negative? Why expect the worst?

She loved what he wanted to do. And maybe she needed to go with that. Go with the positive and focus on making sure he knew how grateful she was.

Moreover, just because this job with him would end didn't necessarily mean she and Jed had to be over, as well. Maybe they could have something good together, something that actually might last.

And a girl never got what she wanted by refusing to try for it, did she? Yes, she'd made a lot of mistakes. But the whole point was to learn from your mistakes, learn and move on, not let them paralyze you, not let them cut you off from the good things that might come your way.

Jed looked really worried now. "You're so quiet. That's not good, is it? Are you pissed at me? Just tell me."

How had this happened? She wasn't quite sure. But she could no longer deny the truth. She was falling for her crazy, knife-wielding, macho-man boss.

She stepped in closer to him. "I, um…"

He fell back. "What? Tell me. God, what?"

Go for it. Stop stalling.

And she did. She stepped right up to him again, lifted

her hands and laid them against his broad, hard chest. The pad and pencil were in the way, but not too much.

Heat flared in those beautiful eyes—and then he turned wary again. "Elise. What the hell?"

"I love it, Jed, that you're building Wigs a catio."

"You do?"

"It's a wonderful idea. Thank you."

"Ahem. Well, okay, then. You're welcome."

"And there's something else…"

"What?" The single word was weighted with suspicion.

Make your move, girl. Do it now.

She slid her hands up to clasp his neck and jumped, lifting her legs and wrapping them around him, hooking her booted feet at his back, letting out a silly "whoops" as she dropped the pad and pencil to the grass in the process.

"Elise!" He caught her automatically, big hands so warm and strong, cradling her thighs. "What in the…?"

She answered the question he couldn't quite seem to ask by threading her fingers up into his thick hair and guiding him down until his mouth finally crashed into hers.

Chapter Six

Jed wasn't sure exactly how this had happened.

He only knew he liked it. A lot.

Her mouth felt like heaven, soft and so willing. Exactly as he'd always imagined it might. He nudged at her parted lips until she opened wider on a sweet little moan. And he dipped his tongue deeper, into honeyed wetness, retreating only in order to catch her plump lower lip between his teeth.

Amazing.

He hadn't expected this. No way.

Apparently, the catio had been a very good idea.

She was grateful. And willing to show it—with that wide, sweet mouth of hers and those full, smooth thighs.

Elise, wrapped all around him. Talk about a red-letter day.

She tasted so good, like apples and honey, and she

smelled like clean cotton warmed by the sun. She moaned some more and wriggled against him, causing fine flares of heat to chase across his skin everywhere her curvy body rubbed his. He was already hard, aching. And it was good.

So good. Those full, soft breasts smashed against his chest, the hot notch between her thighs rubbing him right where he wanted her most.

Since the night the cat got out, he'd been considering how and when to make his move.

Leave it to Elise to make his move for him—and so enthusiastically, too.

Elise all over him. Did it get any better?

Yeah. Yeah, it did.

When he had her naked, that would be even better. And right now, judging by her kiss and her hot little sighs, he knew they would get there. He would have her in his bed minus all her clothes. He groaned at the thought of it.

Life was good. His book was coming together and Elise would be coming apart for him. Soon. Tonight.

He had no complaints. Not a one.

He had those pretty legs wrapped around him now, had her mouth fused to his as she rubbed herself against him.

Things were working out just right—or they were until she fisted her fingers in his hair and pulled her mouth away from his.

He let out a growl of protest. "Get back here."

She laughed, the sound low and way too damn sexy. "Let's not get carried away."

"Why not? Getting carried away sounds like a fine plan to me."

She kissed him again, a quick, hard press of her soft lips to his, the feeling so sweet—and over much too soon. "Let me down," she commanded.

Against his better judgment, he obeyed, another groan breaking from him as she slid along the front of him. Once she had boots on the ground, she offered that mouth again. He took it, hard and deep, kissing her for all he was worth, hoping that if he did a bang-up job of it, she wouldn't ever pull away.

But then she did. Damn it.

Dropping back onto her heels, she stared up at him dreamily. "We should get back. Nell is coming for dinner and your pages for the afternoon are not going to write themselves."

He touched her hair, because he could, because he'd wanted to for way too long and now was his chance. It was so warm under his hand. He couldn't wait to spear his fingers into it, rub the smooth strands against his mouth, his belly and even lower. "I want more. More of you. More of this…"

Those dark eyes were so serious. "Me, too." Her lips were flushed a deeper red from his kiss. He wanted to taste them again. "But we need to talk first."

What was it with women and talking first? "Talking's overrated."

Her smile bloomed—a little bit patient, a little bit tender and more than a little bit exasperated. "We would be changing everything up after you made it so painfully clear that first day. Strictly professional, wasn't that what you said?"

"I've rethought that."

"Jed. Are you sure?"

"Oh, hell, yes." He took her by the shoulders, pulled

her up tight against him and claimed that fine mouth one more time. He made this one last. But eventually, she pulled away again.

Sighing, she stared up at him, dreamier than ever, her red mouth still parted. "I can't think straight when you kiss me."

"Good. I like you like this—soft, unfocused. I like it a lot. You should be like this often, preferably while naked in my bed."

She blinked and her gaze sharpened. "I was so sure a few minutes ago."

"About…?"

"This. Us. But then it always comes back around to what if we go for it and it screws everything up?"

"There's no what-if about this. We're going for it. And nothing's getting screwed up. You're too tough and determined for that."

She hummed low in her throat. "I could say the same about you."

"Exactly. You want this job and I want you doing this job. That won't change."

He got a firm nod for that. "Until this book of yours is done."

And the next one. And the one after that. But she wasn't ready to go there yet.

So he offered her his hand. She bent and grabbed the pencil and steno pad from the tall grass. Then she slipped her fingers in his and they started back down the path.

Nell showed up right on time that night. She took a beer and she showed them the plans she'd drawn up. They looked great to Jed.

He suggested a few more catwalks, a cozy cat house and a half roof projecting off the house instead of all wire fencing overhead. "That way he can go out no matter what the weather's like."

"You got it." Nell made notes of the changes.

"It's fabulous," said Elise. Her cheeks were flushed with pleasure. She was bent over the table admiring Nell's sketches and she looked across at him and mouthed, *Thank you.* She really did seem grateful.

Too bad he'd invited Nell to stay for dinner. He wanted to hustle Elise's sister out the door and get on with the evening, just the two of them alone.

But it turned out okay. Elise seemed really happy to have her sister there. The two of them talked family stuff. Their brother Carter was marrying his fiancée and business partner, Paige Kettleman, on the second Saturday in August. And their brother James's wife, Addie, was expecting her first baby in October. The Bravo women were planning a shower for her.

Nell asked him how the book was going.

"Great," he answered honestly. "Ever since your sister showed up at my door."

Nell left at 2100 hours. Elise walked her out. Jed had just loaded the last dish and shut the dishwasher door when she joined him in the kitchen.

She folded her arms across her beautiful breasts and braced a hip against the granite counter. "Thanks. For giving Wigs a designer-quality outdoor space. For inviting my sister to dinner."

He straightened to his height. "Just keep wearing those little Daisy Duke cutoffs and whatever you want, it's yours."

She glanced down at her cowboy boots and then back

up at him. And then she started in about his books, of all things. "As of last night, I've read all five Jack Mc-Cannon novels—well, actually, I listened to them in audiobook. In the bathtub."

Elise in the bathtub. Now there was an image to conjure with. He needed to be closer to her. It was a physical imperative. He left the dishwasher behind and joined her at the corner of the center island. "All five. Impressive."

"I enjoyed them." She tipped her face up to him. Like an offering, he decided. He was just about to take her mouth, when she said, "Jack is endlessly resourceful. Always coming up with new ways to kill people."

He raised a hand and brushed his fingers over the plump curve of her cheek. He needed more contact, so he smoothed a hand down her hair. It wasn't enough. So he lowered his mouth to hers.

The kiss was slow. Exploratory. She tasted of coffee and the raspberry gelato Deirdre had left them for dessert.

When he lifted his head, she said breathlessly, "Jack needs a real girlfriend."

"Oh, does he?"

"Mmm-hmm. He needs to get beyond the endless chain of gorgeous and potentially deadly hookups, you know?"

He slipped a hand under the warm fall of her hair and cupped the nape of her neck. "You're nervous."

"Yeah?" She made it a question. It was adorable.

He bent a little closer and whispered, "You don't really want to talk about work, do you?"

Her very kissable mouth trembled. "Why not? You love your work."

"At the moment—" he kissed one soft cheek "—work is the last thing on my mind." He kissed the other cheek. "But okay. You say Jack needs a girlfriend. I'm not completely averse to the idea. A man gets tired of bed-hopping after a while."

"And for Jack, it's worse."

"Because?"

"He's bed-hopping while the bullets are flying. He must be exhausted."

"You think you're cute." He kissed the tip of her nose. "It's okay. You are."

Her cheeks flushed the prettiest shade of pink. "She should be someone…unexpected. Someone who doesn't fit into his world. But maybe someone who turns out to be just as resourceful as he is in her own special way."

"I like that."

"I think it could be good. I think it could bring a whole new dimension to the, uh…" Her voice faded away as he ran the backs of his fingers down the side of her throat. He considered kissing her there, using his teeth a little, making a mark. "Jed?"

"Hmm?"

"How many women have you been with?"

"Several. And do you really want to talk about that now?"

"I don't know what happened. I was so confident this afternoon, but tonight…"

He bent close and brushed his lips against her hair just over her ear. "Tell me."

"Well, for some reason, now I just feel so…scared."

"Of me?" He bent and kissed that tempting spot on the side of her throat. A sweet shudder went through her. He scraped his teeth there, too—but very lightly. She shuddered again.

"Not really of you—but a *little* of you." Her voice had a slight tremor. "We have it all worked out, you know? It's all going so well. There's a…a balance of power. I'm afraid that you and me, like this, will put us all out of whack."

"It won't." He brushed his mouth up over her chin and settled his lips on hers again. "You taste so good." He breathed the words against her mouth.

"I've never been, well, particularly sexy, you know?"

He kissed one cheek and then the other and then her mouth again. "What idiot told you that?"

"Nobody had to tell me. I know exactly who I am, what I'm like. I'm…kind of fussy. Controlling. I like things a certain way. Men want me to take care of them when they're down. But nobody finds me especially exciting."

"They're blind. All of them. Luckily for you, you ran into me."

"Oh, don't be silly."

He caught her face between his hands and waited for her to look up at him. When she finally did, he said, "I am never silly."

She let out a gusty sigh. "I'm the kind of girl a guy comes to when he's in trouble, when he needs comfort. I'm the dependable type. A guy can come to my place—before it burned down, I mean—and I would cook him an excellent dinner. And until my recent financial crisis, I was always good for a loan if a guy was broke."

He nuzzled her hair aside and caught her earlobe between his teeth. "I don't need a loan, but you can cook for me anytime."

"And that's another thing…" She gasped as he took her by the waist and lifted her. "Jed!" She clutched at his shoulders. "What are you doing?"

He plunked her down on the island. "Getting eye-to-eye."

She shivered. "This granite is cold."

He nudged her thighs apart and stepped between them. "Let me heat you up." He got right to work on that, using his palms, rubbing her bare thighs in long, lingering strokes.

She laughed then, a sweet and nervous sound. "You never give up, do you?"

"Not a chance. What other thing?" When she frowned in puzzlement, he reminded her, "I said you can cook for me anytime, and you said 'that's another thing.'"

"Oh, right…" She chewed the corner of her lip, her eyes wide and anxious.

"Well?" He bent forward just enough to kiss the tip of her nose again.

"I probably shouldn't admit it…"

"Of course you should. Tell me."

"Well, speaking of food, the truth is I've put on some weight since I lost everything."

"Have you, now?"

"Sometimes it takes a lot of donuts to make a girl forget her troubles."

"And to that I have to say, thank God for donuts."

She wrinkled her nose at him. "What does that even mean?"

"It means the donuts look good on you and you should keep eating them."

"You don't really mean that."

"Elise. You ought to know me well enough by now

to realize that I don't bother to say things I don't mean. I like a woman to be womanly. Curvy. Soft."

"Well, I'm certainly that these days."

"Oh, yes you are." He cradled her face between his palms and stole yet another kiss. She sighed against his lips and then opened for him.

For a little while, except for the occasional soft, urgent moan, the kitchen was quiet. He unbuttoned her shirt, taking his time about it, working his way down, until the shirt was open and he could slip his hand inside, where she was so soft and perfect.

He cradled her breast, finding her nipple hidden under the lace. He flicked it with his thumb, enjoying the way it hardened into a tight little knot. At the same time, he trailed his mouth downward over her chin, her throat, to the two pretty points of her collarbone. He scraped his teeth against those.

She whispered his name then… "Jed…" It sounded so good, his name on her lips, a breathless, hungry little cry. The woman got him hard without even trying to. He took her lips again. "Jed…" She said it into his mouth that time. He drank it right down.

So good, the fresh, clean scent of her, turning musky and mouthwatering as he stroked her bare thighs and rubbed at her soft belly and then slipped his fingers around to unhook the clasp of her bra.

"Oh!" she cried. "I know what you're doing, Jed," she scolded as the clasp gave way.

He chuckled, something he didn't do every day. Then he eased her shirt off her plump shoulders and peeled off her bra. Now, he had her naked from the waist up and he felt really good about that.

Until she suddenly rediscovered the concept of modesty and brought up her arms to cover those round, ripe breasts he'd been waiting to see for weeks now. "Don't do it, Elise." He caught her wrists, one and then the other, and guided them back down. "Hold on to the counter."

She let out a low whimper of sound, but she did what he told her to.

He went to work on the cutoffs, undoing the metal button at the top, sliding the zipper down. Her little panties were pink. She wouldn't have them on for long.

"Lie back," he instructed.

"This is very unsanitary. Jed, we eat lunch here."

"Shh. Lie back."

"Oh, dear…" But she did it, went over onto her back. She stared up at the beamed ceiling and whispered, "This is so not me."

"Elise." He stroked both palms down one glorious thigh, over her knee and her calf to her boot. "Take my word for it." He pulled off the boot and dropped it to the floor. "It's you."

He took the other boot next, and then the little yellow socks she wore underneath them.

"So pretty." He moved in close again, bending over her where she was spread out on the counter, his own personal feast. He cupped both of her full breasts, one in either hand. All soft and white, they just happened to fit his palms exactly right. And then he spent a few minutes kissing her pretty pink nipples, taking turns on one and then the other, until she couldn't hold back her moans and she lifted her hips to him, rocking, begging him with that lush body of hers to give her more.

He had more for her.

He had lots and lots more.

The Daisy Duke cutoffs had to go next. He hooked his fingers under the waistband on either side. "Lift up."

She whimpered in protest. But she lifted. He whipped them down and tossed them away. He left her the panties, for the moment. They were so innocent and pink and he wanted to look at them, wanted to play with her through the cotton and lace.

He took her hips and pulled her right to the edge of the counter, moving in good and close, so his body opened her legs for him. And then he bent over her again.

"Jed, I…"

"Shh…" So much to enjoy. He hardly knew where to start.

He got to work, kissing. Touching. Biting a little, exploring the sweet, shadowed places—behind her ear, along the lush under curves of her breasts. And lower.

Her belly called his name. He answered with his lips, his tongue, the edges of his teeth, dipping into her navel, biting the beautiful rounded curve below it.

She wiggled and moaned and then whimpered, "Jed?"

"Hmm?"

"Do you have, you know, condoms?"

"I do."

"I keep thinking this is a bad idea."

"Thinking." He dropped a line of kisses along the lacy top edge of her panties. "That's your problem. You shouldn't be thinking. Stop."

"But I—"

"Shh…" He put his open mouth against her mound, right over the pink cotton that covered her from his sight.

"Oh, my goodness…"

He had to agree. The scent of her alone was pure heaven. A man could die happy with the smell of her around him. He drew in a big breath and he released it against the pink-covered core of her.

"I... Oh! Oh, my!"

"Baby, you are the hottest thing." He kept kissing her, breathing against her, heating her further through her little pink panties.

"But I'm not, I... Oh. My. Golly." She speared her fingers in his hair. "Oh, now that! Jed!"

"Hmm?"

"Yes! Please! That."

He chuckled again. Tonight he was a chuckling fool. He ached to have her, to just tear those panties right off, rip his fly wide and bury himself in her, hard and deep.

But half the fun was making it last, driving both of them crazy, making both of them burn. He slid his hand up her thigh again as she wriggled and moaned for him. "Wet," he whispered against her core, easing a finger in under the elastic, then nudging it aside farther with his nose. Silky. Hot. Dripping with need. "So wet, sweetheart. So fine..."

She clutched at his shoulders. "I never get like this..."

"You do now. And I like you like this. I like it a lot." And enough with the panties. Now they were just in his way. He used both hands, taking one side and then the other, tearing them at the seams, ripping them away.

With a sharp gasp, she lifted her head off the counter and accused, "You just ruined my panties."

"Sorry, beautiful." He tossed the torn pink scraps over his shoulder. "They had to go. Now, where was I?"

"Oh, my goodness..." She let her head fall back.

And he lifted her thighs, hooked them over his shoulders and bent to his work. She was so wet and open and ready, slick and eager, defenseless against him. He tasted her deeply, using his fingers, too, as she rocked and moaned and pulled at his hair. She was sweet and salty on his tongue, drenched and so willing now, opening her legs wider as he kissed her. She'd flown right past her own objections. She was no longer afraid.

She offered him everything, all of her.

He would definitely take that: all of Elise.

"Oh!" she cried again and pumped her hips faster, letting her thighs fall open even wider, bracing her feet on his back. He speared his tongue in, stroked her faster and deeper with his fingers and stuck with her as she climbed toward the finish.

When she shattered, he held on, riding it out with her, drinking her sweetness as she chanted his name.

Chapter Seven

Several minutes passed.

Elise was gone. Done. Finished. She felt as though she'd left her body behind, as though she floated near the ceiling, that she was nothing but a moonbeam, a thoroughly satisfied shimmer of pale, vibrant light.

Except, wait. No. She was very much in her body. She felt every inch of her own skin, every bit of her that Jed had stroked and kissed and driven to the kind of spinning, churning, mind-altering climax she'd only read about in books.

From some brave space within her, she gathered all her courage and lifted her head.

Jed, way down there between her still-open legs, looked up from the cradle of her thighs. His face was wet. From her. "So good," he said, and he bent close again to place three kisses—on her left thigh, then her right and finally on that place in the center where he'd just rocked her world. "Beard burn." He brushed more kisses on the scruff-red skin of her unabashedly open thighs. "Sorry…"

"Don't be." She reached down and touched his hair again, so thick and coarse against her fingertips. "It's kind of tingly. Feels good." Her legs were shaking a little. She eased them off his shoulders, put her arm across her eyes and indulged in a moan of total disbelief. "On the kitchen counter, no less. This can't be real."

"Sweetheart, take my word for it. This is as real as it gets." He rose from between her thighs and then bent over her. He pressed a kiss just below her navel. She lowered her arm to look at him again. "And we are not done yet," he said, his voice a low rumble, barely a whisper, deliciously rough. "Not by a long shot." He kissed his way upward along her body until they were face-to-face. "We're going up to my room now."

"Oh, I don't know if we really ought to do that."

"*I* know. We're going." He took her hand and pulled her to a sitting position. Then he clasped her waist and helped her down to the floor.

She looked around at her boots and her socks, her shirt, her cutoffs and her torn underpants all strewn across the floor. "I feel really, really bare right about now."

"It's a great look for you—and don't even think about trying to cover up."

"Let me at least pick up my—"

"Nope." He stopped her with a hand on her shoulder. "We're going upstairs and we're going now."

"Easy for you to say. You've still got all your clothes on, but I'm supposed to bounce through the house buck naked."

"I'm going to let go." He squeezed her shoulder. "Don't you dare move a muscle."

"I don't see why we have to—"

"Don't. Move." He said it in his master-of-the-universe voice.

And then he let go of her—and stripped. She stood there and stared with her mouth hanging open. He did it so fast, dropping everything to the floor where he stood.

And did he ever look good when he was done. There wasn't an inch of him that wasn't buff and hard and honed to perfection. He was fully erect. And large. Very large.

She gulped.

He said, "It's going to be fine, Elise. Better than fine. You do it for me in a big way and I'm not letting you out of my arms for the rest of the night." And then he grabbed her and scooped her high against his chest. He didn't even grunt at the effort.

She linked her hands behind his neck. "You'll probably get a hernia hauling me up the stairs."

"Shut up and enjoy the ride." He said it so tenderly, the way another, gentler man might declare undying love.

With a sigh of surprisingly happy surrender, she wrapped her arms around his neck and tucked her head under his chin.

His room was even bigger than hers. It took up half of the second floor and had tall windows on three walls. There was a sitting area the size of a giant living room, complete with a big-screen TV and a fireplace of volcanic-looking rock with an enormous rough-hewn slab of wood for a mantel. The bed was on the same grand scale as the rest of the suite, with a roughly carved headboard, the bedding in brown, black and bronze.

But they didn't make it to the bed.

Not right away, anyway. Jed carried her over the threshold, knocked the door shut with his heel and then let her down to the rug, which was thick and fur-like and covered most of the floor. She was barely on her feet before he was hauling her close again, kissing her deeply. She could feel him, every inch of him, hard and hot along the front of her, his erection pressing into her belly.

How did he do it? She'd never considered herself a particularly sexual person. Letting go wasn't easy for her. Her mind wouldn't stop working. She obsessed over really unsexy stuff—like what if they got fluids on the comforter and why hadn't she thought ahead to grab a towel?

But with Jed, it was different. With Jed, she'd just experienced the best climax of her life. Because he stayed with her; he refused to give up on her. When she'd fretted about the extra weight she'd put on, he called her perfect, soft and curvy and womanly. If she complained because he ripped her panties, he simply said those panties had to go and then put his mouth where she'd never liked any man to kiss her—and blew her mind.

The man had focus in all things.

Including having sex.

And somehow, he got her to focus, too, got her to center her mind down to her senses, to revel in the feel of his big, hard hands on her soft flesh, to glory in the wonder of his hot mouth opening on hers.

The kiss at the door went on and on, his tongue playing with hers, his teeth nipping at her lower lip.

He stroked those big hands along her back, tracing the bumps of her spine. He took a fistful of her hair and pulled on it slowly, insistently, until the kiss broke and she let her head fall back.

He growled low in his throat, a hungry sound, as though he wanted to take a big bite out of her. And then he did take a bite, more or less. He bent his head to her, latched on to the side of her neck and began sucking rhythmically.

Oh, my goodness gracious. She felt that sharp kiss so deep inside, as though a shimmering hot thread connected them, from his wet mouth through her eager flesh and down into the core of her. She ached with wanting. And what she wanted was for him never to stop.

She knew she would have a bruise there. So what? She loved it—loved the sting of his teeth, the warmth of his breath, the stroke of his tongue, soothing her and simultaneously stirring up sparks of sensation that made her shiver. And burn.

And when he clasped her shoulders and gently pushed her down, she didn't even hesitate. She went to her knees on the thick, fluffy rug, opened her eyes and gazed happily up over the thick, ready length of him.

Green eyes gleamed down at her. "Taste me."

Elise didn't hesitate. She made no excuses, didn't fall all over herself explaining that she wasn't any good at going down on a guy.

She didn't have to make excuses. Not with Jed. She just stuck out her tongue and licked him, a long, slow stroke, following the ridge of that thick, twisty vein from the base to the tip, where a pearl of moisture gleamed.

She licked that up, too. It tasted like the wind off the ocean, musky and fresh at the same time.

"Elise," he said. *Elise*, as though her name felt so good on his tongue he wanted to roll it around in his mouth for a while. His fingers grazed her cheek, wandered to her temple, combed through her hair. "More, sweetheart. Please."

So she gave him more. She reached up and wrapped her hand around him. He groaned at that. And then she opened her mouth and took him in.

He didn't fit. But she did her best and he wasn't complaining. He only said, "Harder. Tighter. That's it…"

She took him in and let him out, sucking him back again, using her hands to stroke him, to make him say her name like it was the only name he'd ever known, to wrap his big fingers around the back of her head, cradling her, guiding her…

Until he swore low and commanded, "Stop. Or I'll lose it," which sounded like a fine idea to her.

But he wasn't having that. He caught her face between his hands and his eyes were twin green flames burning down at her. "Come up here. Come on…"

She went, gathering her shaky legs under her and rising. He took her shoulders, steadying her. And then he kissed her, his tongue spearing in, tasting her so deeply, so thoroughly, that her knees grew weak again and threatened to give way.

Before they did, he lifted her and took her to the bed, where he laid her down so gently, you'd think she was fragile, some tender, young breakable thing.

She waited, gazing up at him, loving the sheer masculine beauty of him as he opened the bedside drawer, took out a condom, unwrapped it and rolled it down over his thick, hard length.

Sheathed, he just stood there, watching her as she

watched him. "Look at you," he said in that low voice that promised an endless array of impossible delights. "I could gobble you up, just start with your pretty pink-painted toes and keep going until I had every inch of you."

In her life, she'd felt attractive now and then. Kind of pretty, maybe, at times. But never had she felt truly beautiful.

Not until that moment. When Jed Walsh stared down at her spread out on his bed and said he could eat her right up.

He came down to her and took her in those hard, hot arms, kissing her, touching her, his hands gliding over her, both possessive and tender. Sliding a knee between her legs, he eased her thighs wider, making room to settle himself between them.

She took his weight with a willing sigh. And then he was reaching down, clasping her under her knees, guiding her legs up to wrap around him.

Once he had her as he wanted her, he levered up on his arms, framed her face between his hands and kissed her some more. Oh, she could feel him there, nudging her right where she wanted him.

"Jed. Jed, please…" And she reached down between them, wrapping her fingers around him to guide him in.

He didn't get far.

"Tight." He buried his head against her throat and groaned the word onto her skin. "And perfect. So hot and wet…"

She whispered, "Jed," and added a soft, pleading "yes" for good measure. It had been a long time for her, not since Sean, her last bad boyfriend, almost two years ago now. But she was burning—burning for Jed, wanting him, all of him, and wanting him now.

Still, he was careful. He took it slowly, by aching degrees, stretching her, filling her, stopping after each gentle thrust to give her body a chance to accept him, to make the transition from discomfort to fullness to outright pleasure.

At last, she had him all the way.

He was so still then, so still and so deep within her, filling her completely.

"Jed. Please…" She tried to move.

"Don't," he commanded. "Wait."

"I can't…"

"You will."

"I need…"

"I know."

She was breathing so hard, needing to move with every nerve in her body.

And then, at last, he did move; he withdrew. She moaned, frantic. Afraid she would lose him. But he gave one of those rare, rough chuckles of his and came back to her.

After that, it was so right, a rising wave of sensation. A river of it, flowing through her, into him and back to her again. It started slow and deep and then it was faster.

Harder.

He sat up, pulling her with him. And she was in his lap, her legs around his waist, her feet hooked at his back. She was moving on him, frantic and needful—then sighing and slow. He said things, raw things that only drove her higher, only made it better.

Hotter.

Deeper.

And then he said, "Now, Elise." Only that, only *now* and then her name.

It was all she needed. Her climax rolled through her, violent and beautiful. It lifted her so high and sent her tumbling. There was a shiver of hot light behind her eyes. She felt him go over, felt him pulsing inside her as she hit the peak and began the slow, weightless glide back into herself.

When she came back to the real world again, she was still sitting on his lap, her legs and arms twined around him.

He brushed his lips against her cheek. "Come on, now," he said and carefully guided her to stretch out with him, so they lay on their sides facing each other, her right leg draped across his thigh.

He was still inside her. She wondered how he'd managed to get them down to the pillows without slipping free. The guy kind of amazed her. He had more moves than his alter ego, Jack.

And speaking of moves, she needed to get going, get back to her own room. Maybe he would let her borrow a T-shirt or something. Really, she should have insisted on bringing her clothes when she let him carry her up here.

He put his big hand on the side of her head. "You still with me?"

"Of course." She tried on a smile. It only wobbled a little. "But I should get going, huh?"

"No, you shouldn't." He said it chidingly, and he stroked the hair back from her temple. "You're staying here with me tonight."

No, she wasn't. She needed to get back to her own room. She needed a little distance now, needed some time to herself to…regroup.

She chewed the corner of her lip as she tried to decide what to say.

But he spoke first. "I'm going to go and get rid of this condom." He bent close for a sweet little kiss. Her heart felt like a giant toothache, throbbing away in the cage of her chest. "Do not leave this bed while I'm gone."

"Look, Jed—"

"I'm going to need your word on that, Elise."

Well, okay. Now that she thought about it, she had to admit it would be beyond tacky to just get up and get the hell out the minute he left the room. She might be feeling a little bit shaky now that they'd done…all that they'd done. But she wouldn't just turn tail and run. Or at least, she wouldn't now that he'd gone and busted her on it ahead of time. "Okay. I'll be here."

"That's my girl."

It sounded way too good when he said that. But of course she wasn't really his girl. She needed *not* to make this more than it was.

He kissed her again and then rolled away from her. Rising, he eased off the condom, inspected it for damage and tied it off. Then he turned and started for the bathroom.

She watched him go. He looked so fine. There ought to be a law against a body like his. It really wasn't fair that just looking at that butt of his walking away had her longing to have sex with him all over again.

He disappeared into the other room. As soon as he shut the door, she jumped up, threw back the covers and climbed in between the white sheets. Plumping a couple of pillows at her back, she leaned against the headboard and breathed a sigh of relief as she covered herself.

She'd barely gotten settled when he came back.

He lifted the blankets and slid in beside her, his hard, hairy leg brushing hers as he sat against the headboard, too.

She waited a minute, thinking maybe he would say something first and then, whatever he said, she could just start arguing with it. Because she was not staying here all night. Yes, she was crazy for him. But she really shouldn't have let this happen. She needed this job too much.

And the silence was getting to her. She had to say something. "Look. What just happened was incredible. I, well, I really appreciate it."

"You're welcome," he said drily.

She made herself look at him then, all scruffy and muscled up. How had he gotten so incredibly good-looking? It just wasn't fair. "But seriously, Jed. I need to go back to my room and this can't be happening again."

He took her hand. "It can and it will. Stay."

She looked in those eyes of his and felt foolish. And also inexperienced with men, though she wasn't. She'd had boyfriends. She had experience. And experience had taught her that love didn't work out for her.

Not that this was love. It was way too early to call it anything like that. Yeah, she was falling for him, but how far and how deep remained to be seen.

And that scared the hell out of her. "I just, my life is a mess and this job means everything and I can't afford to be having sex with the boss."

He eased his big arm around her and drew her close to his side. She should pull away. But she didn't. It felt too good to have him hold her. It felt like she mattered to him. That what had happened—on the countertop, in this bed—was a good thing, a natural thing. Not just another stupid move in the never-ending chain of her own bad life decisions. "The boss really, really wants to have sex with you. And the boss sees your value. The last thing he would want to do is drive you away."

"Will you stop talking about yourself in the third person, please? It's kind of creeping me out."

He almost smiled. She could see a little twitch at the corner of that mouth she couldn't help wanting to kiss again. "You've got this job, no matter what happens between the two of us. I would be lost without you—I *was* lost without you. But then you came along and saved my sorry ass. Now Jack McCannon will have book number six and he can give up the endless chain of meaningless hookups and find a real girlfriend. All because of you. There is no way, no matter what happens, that I will ever want you to stop working for me."

She touched his beard-rough jaw in wonder. "Jed. That was beautiful."

He grunted. "I've been told I'm a caveman, but I try."

"I have to point out, though—"

"Of course you do."

She scowled at him. "This isn't funny."

He scowled back. "You're right. I am not laughing. Continue."

"It's just that if you go and break my heart, *I* will want to leave."

"I would never break your heart."

"Well, not that you would want to. But it does happen."

He leaned closer, nuzzled her cheek. "I have a suggestion."

"You are being much too wonderful. You know that, right?"

"It must be your civilizing influence."

"Okay, that's a little *too* wonderful. Dial it back or I'll start thinking you're trying to manipulate me."

"But I am trying to manipulate you—to stay here with me for the rest of the night."

She sighed and laid her head on his shoulder. "Well, guess what? I think it's working."

He pressed his lips into her hair. "Excellent. And how about this? Why don't we just play it by ear and not borrow trouble?"

"But I'm always seeing all the ways things could go wrong. I can't help it. Things *have* gone wrong for me and I just want to keep them from going wrong again."

He trailed his fingers up and down her bare arm. The slow caress soothed her. And excited her at the same time. "Stay with me," he whispered. "Please."

She took his hand, laced their fingers together and rested them against her heart. Because she did want to stay. And clearly, he still wanted her here. Shyly, she admitted, "You're amazingly convincing."

His fingers tightened on hers. "I'm going to consider that a yes."

She snuggled in a little closer. "So. I'm guessing you probably have your own bathtub in here…"

"Yours is bigger than mine," she said with a pout ten minutes later, when they sat in his jetted tub with bubbles all around them.

Jed sat behind her. He had her right where he wanted her, cradled between his legs. She'd piled her hair up and managed to twist it so it stayed on top of her head and she leaned back against him, so soft and sweet, every inch of her a blatant invitation to do more wicked things to her.

"Yes, my tub is bigger," he said. "And if you're very, very nice to me, I will share it with you often."

She wiggled against him. He tried not to groan. "I get the feeling you really do like having me here."

"And soon, I intend to show you how much."

"Um." She tipped her head back and looked up into his eyes. "A name came to me. For Jack's girlfriend? I don't expect you to use it, but I can't resist telling you, anyway."

"Go for it."

"Sadika. Sadika Niles."

He liked it. "It's good. I'm stealing it from you."

She giggled. "You can't steal it. I'm *giving* it to you."

"Thank you—and you're giving me ideas."

She wiggled again. "I can feel them."

"I'm talking about Sadika."

"Yeah. Sure you are."

He put his hands on her shoulders and stroked his way down her bubble-covered arms to her hands. "Sadika Niles is in her thirties. She's black, a surgeon. From a well-to-do family...or wait. A preacher." He wrapped his hands around the back of hers.

"She's a preacher? That's odd." She spread her fingers and he eased his between them.

"Not Sadika, her father. John Niles is a minister. In Biloxi, Mississippi. And Sadika is on duty in the ER at Manhattan General the night the one-handed man, whose name will turn out to be Vanko Tesler, is admitted, near death, after trying and failing to kill Jack. Sadika performs the extensive touch-and-go surgery that saves Tesler. But the next night, when she goes to check on her patient, she witnesses his execution by a hitman sent by K." The mysterious K, an international arms dealer and general scumbag, had appeared in four McCannon books so far.

"So the one-handed man dies?" Idly, she lifted their linked hands from the water. Bubbles slid off before she lowered their arms below the surface again.

He bent close to press a kiss against the side of her neck. "Elise. It's a Jack McCannon novel. A lot of people have to die."

"Mmm." She tipped her head to the side, allowing him better access. He took total advantage of that and nipped gently at her smooth, damp flesh. "Watch it," she warned, but in a low, throaty voice that contradicted her complaint. "I've already got one hickey. I don't need another. Deirdre will wonder what we get up to when she's not around."

He licked where he'd nipped her, caught a loose curl of dark hair and tugged on it with his teeth. "I don't care what Deirdre thinks."

"Well, I do." But then she turned her head enough that he could claim her mouth. They shared a long, lazy kiss, during which he eased his fingers from between hers and put his hands where they longed to be—over her wet, bubble-covered breasts.

"Where was I?" he asked when she turned back around and settled against him again.

She made a sweet little humming sound as he rubbed his thumbs across her hard little nipples. "Sadika witnesses the execution of the one-handed man in his hospital room."

"Right. And Jack finds out there's a witness and he's

there in her apartment when she gets home just before dawn. K's men come for her."

"Jack has to protect her." She laughed in delight. "And they're on the run together. You should have Jack get injured and she has to operate on him under less than optimal conditions."

"Absolutely."

"And maybe Sadika eventually has to kill that sexy assassin, Lilias, in order to protect Jack."

"Hold on. I'm kind of fond of Lilias."

"Well, I'm not. Especially if she goes after Jack, she really needs to die."

He wanted her facing him. So he took her shoulders and floated her around until those glorious breasts were pressed to his chest and his aching erection nudged her belly. "You are a bloodthirsty creature."

Her mouth was a soft O, her eyes low and lazy. "You make me...different. You make me feel things I've never felt before."

"I don't make you anything. You are what you are, Elise. Womanly. Sexy. Smart..." Beneath the bubbles and the cooling water, he traced a finger over the curve of her hip and inward, parting the soft, neatly trimmed hair between her lush thighs.

A moan escaped her. "Again?"

He dipped a finger inside. "Don't pretend you're surprised." And then he claimed that mouth he couldn't get enough of kissing.

A few minutes later, he pulled her out of the tub and licked off the bubbles that cascaded down her luscious wet curves, going to his knees for a while to enjoy the taste of her, then rising, sliding on a condom, backing her to the wall and lifting her. She wrapped those beautiful legs around him and he eased her down onto him.

After that, he kind of lost touch with reality for a while. Her soft heat surrounded him, her scent filled his head and he drank her sweet cries off those lips that whimpered his name as she reached her climax.

A little later, he carried her back to bed, turned off the light and settled her in close to him, her round, soft bottom tucked just right in the cradle of his thighs. He waited until her breathing evened out in sleep before he allowed himself to join her there.

Elise opened her eyes to darkness and the scent of cinnamon: Jed. He was all around her, his huge, heavy arm in the crook of her waist, his big hand cupping one breast. She felt…engulfed by him.

It was far too pleasant a sensation. Arousing, somehow. Her whole body ached. But in a good way. A well-used way.

She could too easily get accustomed to this—to Jed holding her in sleep. To waking up beside him. To plotting his stories while lazing around with him in that giant tub of his.

And to the sex.

Oh, God. The sex. A pleasured flush swept through her just thinking about the things they'd done.

Jed moved. His hand closed a little tighter on her breast. It felt delicious. She almost arched her back to press herself closer to his palm.

But then he let go. His arm left her waist. He rolled away from her.

She lay very still and listened to his breathing. Even and shallow. Sound asleep—and so far away now, turned on his other side across the wide expanse of the bed.

The clock on the nightstand glowed at her—3:10 in the morning. She stared at it as a minute crawled by. And then another and another after that. As she watched the glowing numerals change, all the doubts he'd banished with his wonderfully flattering reassurances came creeping back.

Now, really. Did she honestly want to be here naked in this bed with him when daylight came?

It could be awkward. Awkward and strange and very likely embarrassing. And, well, she just didn't want to deal with that. There was no reason to deal with that. She had a perfectly lovely bed of her own downstairs. She could wake up in the morning in the privacy of her room and pull herself together before having to look in Jed Walsh's green eyes after he'd seen everything she had under her clothes. Seen it up close and from a whole lot of potentially unflattering angles.

Nope. Waking up to daylight in Jed's bed was not going to happen.

Moving at a snail's pace so as not to disturb him, she eased from under the covers, slid her feet to the floor and crept to the door. It opened for her without a sound.

Wigs sat waiting on the other side. "Mrow?"

"Shh, now." She shut the door behind her. Scooping up the cat, she headed for the stairs.

To get to her room, she had to pass the kitchen and the clothes all over the floor in there. Deirdre would be here tomorrow, sometime between eight and nine.

It should be fine. Elise would set the alarm for six and have everything picked up and put away long before the housekeeper arrived.

But after she and Wigs were safely in her room, well, those clothes just nagged at her. She kept flashing on images of Deirdre standing there in the kitchen, blinking in bewilderment at the bra tossed on the island counter, the torn panties on the floor.

So she put on her robe and went back out there. She gathered up Jed's clothes, folded them neatly and set them on the first step of the stairs, his boots beside them. Then she grabbed all of her stuff and took it back to her room.

By then it was twenty minutes to four. She put on some comfy sleep shorts and a frayed racer-back T-shirt, climbed into her bed, pulled the covers over her head and assumed there was no way she would get back to sleep.

But apparently, she dropped off rather quickly.

The next thing she knew Jed was bending over her. Even in the darkness, she could see enough to realize that he didn't have a stitch on. You'd think if he just *had* to break into her room in the middle of the night, he could have put some pants on first. "Elise. What the hell?"

She blinked at her bedside clock. Ten after four. And then she grumbled, "What are you doing in here?"

Apparently, Wigs didn't get it, either. "Mrow?" he asked from the foot of the bed.

Jed didn't bother to answer either her or her cat. He just tossed back the covers, gathered her into his arms and carried her back up the stairs with Wigs following happily along behind.

Chapter Eight

Elise slept in Jed's bed from that night on. Jed made it perfectly clear he wanted her with him. Why try to escape him when she only wanted the same thing?

She knew it wasn't wise or the least bit professional of her, to be the boss's plaything after working hours. She probably ought to be ashamed of herself.

But she wasn't.

She felt much too happy to be ashamed. She loved every minute she spent in his bed. As it turned out, it wasn't awkward or uncomfortable in the least to wake up beside him every morning. He made it crystal clear that he liked waking up with her there. Opening her eyes to morning light with Jed wrapped all around her? She'd never had it so good.

And making love with him just kept getting better. Every time she had sex with him, it was the best of her life.

So far.

With Jed, she shed her inhibitions along with her clothes. He made her feel like a goddess in bed. And after a lifetime of considering herself boring, fussy and repressed, seeing herself through Jed's eyes was pretty darn fabulous. Whatever happened in the end, how could she regret spending her nights with a smoking hot man's man who thought she was sex on a stick?

She worried a little in the initial few days of being his lover that his writing might suffer and he would rethink the wisdom of boinking his assistant, that he would tell her they had to go back to how it had been before.

But no. On the contrary, his book seemed to be going better than ever.

He said she inspired him, that the story just flowed. He claimed it was a lot because of Sadika, whom he'd introduced the morning after that first night. Sadika was turning out to be strong, sharp-tongued and capable, a woman even the great Jack McCannon didn't dare mess with. Jed thought Sadika brought out a whole other side of Jack—the dark side, where his heart lay hidden. Jed said he hadn't realized that Jack was getting a little stale until Sadika showed up and Jack had skin in the game again, someone who mattered, someone worth fighting for.

More than once in the two weeks after he first tore her panties off, Jed carried her upstairs during writing hours. She got lucky each time and Deirdre didn't spot them. Elise knew it was cowardly of her, to want to keep the personal side of their relationship strictly between them. But so what? She just wasn't ready for anyone else to know.

And sex during working hours? With Jed, it was

every bit as amazing as sex any other time. Just a little more urgent, somehow. They would make love hard and fast and then they would talk. About the story, about whatever element wasn't quite working. He said she was a great sounding board. He liked to bounce ideas off her, find out what she thought of them, get her take on how he might resolve any problems that cropped up.

She really liked hashing out story points. She could do that forever—unlike the typing, which she couldn't be finished with soon enough. When Jed completed this book, she would miss a lot about being involved in his writing process. But typing? If she never typed another sentence, it would be much too soon.

Nell and crew showed up the last Tuesday in July to begin construction on the catio. Elise took special care when her sister was there not to give Jed any smoldering looks, not to stand too close to him and definitely never to touch him. She did not want her sister to know that there was anything more than work going on between her and her boss. If Elise and Jed were still together when the book was through and she returned to her own life, that would be the time to let her family know that they were an item.

Bravo Construction did good work and they did it quickly. A week later, Mr. Wiggles had his own personal backyard. He loved it. He climbed the cat runs and hid in the hidey-holes, basked in the August sun and stalked the birds that flitted beyond the wire fencing.

Besides the fire pit and the Adirondack chairs, Jed had decided to add a comfy outdoor living room to the patio. He'd also had Nell install a fancy grill and a sink and counter space—essentially an outdoor kitchen. That way, after work, they could join Wigs outside.

The first Friday in August, Jed grilled chicken out there and Elise baked potatoes and whipped up a salad. They sat down to eat at the cast-iron table not far from the fire pit.

Elise was spooning sour cream onto her potato when he asked, "So what's on your mind?"

She plunked the spoon back in the tub of sour cream. "What do you mean?"

He shrugged. "Just now you were biting your lip. And you keep shooting me glances when you think I'm not looking. You're building up to hitting me with something and you're not sure how to go about it."

How did he do it? He read her like a billboard. Sometimes that made her feel special and important to him. Sometimes, like now, she had to tamp down annoyance that he found her so transparent. "My half brother Carter is getting married a week from Saturday."

"I know. You and Nell talked about the wedding that night she came for dinner."

"I need the afternoon off so that I can be there— and yes, when you hired me I agreed to work all day, every day, six days a week. I should have asked for my brother's wedding day then, but I had a lot on my mind and I just didn't think of it. Then, later, I kept putting off asking because I was afraid you'd say no and, given our agreement, you would be perfectly within your rights to say no and then I would have to decide whether or not to make some sort of stand about it. And then we made love and now I'm sleeping with you and I feel like I would be taking advantage of our intimate relationship to ask you—"

"Enough." He waved a chicken leg at her. "It's not

a problem. We're ahead on the book. Take the whole day off."

She picked up her fork and set it down without using it. "Seriously? I've got the whole day? Just like that?"

He nodded. She was about to leap up, run around the table and grab him in a grateful hug when he added, "Will I need to wear a tux, or what?" She sank back into her chair. Being Jed, he only had to look at her face to know what she was thinking. "So. You weren't planning on taking me."

"Well, Jed, it's only that I…" Ugh. Whatever she said next, it wouldn't sound good.

"I'm waiting, Elise. That sentence is never going to finish itself."

She let out a hard breath, sucked in another one and tried again. "If you go with me, my family will know that we're seeing each other—I mean, you know, dating, or whatever. That I'm not just your assistant, you know?"

"Yes, Elise. I do know. And you're *not* just my assistant. You're…" He let the word trail off as he drank from his water glass and set it back down with care. "What shall we call you? I don't especially like the word *girlfriend*. It's weak. *Lover* sounds vaguely reprehensible. And this isn't just an added-benefits situation, either. It's more."

"Well, yes, what we have is really good and I love it, Jed. I love being with you, I truly do, but—"

"What you are, Elise, is mine. My woman. And my woman does not go to her half brother's wedding—or anyone's wedding, for that matter—without me."

Her panties were suddenly wet. He went all caveman on her and she loved it. But still. She didn't want her family to know that she spent her nights in his arms. Not yet, anyway. It was much too soon to be anybody's business but hers and Jed's. "If my family knows that I'm more than just your assistant, they're going to worry about me. You know I've made bad choices. They know it, too. I just don't want to deal with that."

"Deal with what, exactly?"

"Oh, come on. Most of the time you read my mind, but now I have to draw you a picture?"

"Just say it, Elise."

"Fine. I can't deal with knowing that *they* know I'm sleeping with the boss."

"But you *are* sleeping with the boss. It's a fact. And you just said that it's damn good between us. It's nothing to be ashamed of."

She couldn't hold back a pained cry. "You don't know them. They're so protective—especially of me since I screwed up my life. At least one of my brothers is going to get you aside and tell you that you'd better treat me right, or else."

"Well, I do treat you right and I'm happy to tell your brothers that I do. No problem."

"And Nell. God, who knows what Nellie will do? I love her and I'm grateful for all the ways she's got my back. But she thinks she's big mama grizzly or something. She'll be threatening to kick your ass if you break my heart."

He waved a hand. "It's not a big deal. Nell has already threatened to kick my ass in regards to you. Twice."

She wanted to scream. "Excuse me? I didn't know that. Why don't I know that? You never said a word about it."

"I knew it would only freak you out and I was happy to reassure your sister. End of story."

"When?" she demanded.

"'When' what?"

"When did my sister threaten to kick your ass?"

"The first time was when I called her and asked her to make this cat patio."

"What? No, she didn't. We weren't even sleeping together then."

"Yes, she did. And no, we weren't. That time she only meant I'd better treat you right on the job."

"Oh, great. Fabulous."

"The second time was a week ago, after she and her crew had been working on the patio for three days. She called me outside under the pretense of approving some tweak she'd made to the outdoor kitchen layout. I joined her by the grill, at which point she grabbed my arm, dragged me into the trees and said she wasn't an idiot and it was crystal clear to her that you were doing more for me than typing my book."

Elise facepalmed. "Just shoot me now."

Jed went right on. "She threatened to make a eunuch of me if I ever made you cry. I reminded her that you were a hell of a woman and thus bound to cry now and then. I told her I planned always to be there to dry your tears."

Elise lifted her face from her hands. "You did? You do?" Now she definitely felt like crying.

"Yeah."

"How can you say such wonderful things?"

"One, I mean them. Two, I have a certain facility with words."

She blinked away the tears and sat up straighter.

"It's beautiful, what you just said. But I really think I need to remind you that it's much too early to be saying such things to other people, even my sister, about you and me."

His sexy mouth twitched at the corner. "I didn't know there was a schedule I was supposed to be following."

"It's only been two and a half weeks since that first time. We shouldn't rush into anything."

"I'm not rushing anywhere. I'm right where I want to be."

"And I'm glad." Her throat clutched with emotion. "I'm where I want to be, too." Her food was getting cold. She picked up a chicken thigh and had a bite, then she ate some of her potato.

"Elise." His voice had that tone. Absolute and unwavering. "You're not going to that wedding without me."

She wanted to cry again. "If Nell knows, Jody knows. And Clara, too, probably. And maybe my cousin Rory. And possibly Chloe, my half brother Quinn's wife. All my brothers probably know too, by now."

"So it's a done deal. Move on."

"Easy for you to say. You're not the family screwup."

"You're no screwup. Your family loves you and that makes them protective of you. And you're far too proud for your own good." He said it softly. Tenderly. And that made her want to go jump in his lap, wrap her arms good and tight around his neck and beg him to take her to bed right this minute. But then he added, "And you can look at it this way. If I don't go with you, they're all going to think you mean so little to me that I didn't even bother to take you to Carter's wedding. Your brothers will beat the crap out of me and Nell will cut off my—"

"Stop it. All right. I give."

He sent a glance heavenward. "Finally."

"You won't need a tux. A suit or a sport coat and slacks will be fine. It's outdoors. One of those scenic wedding venues not far out of town."

He gave her a look that smoldered and teased at the same time. "You haven't even asked me yet."

"Right. A minute ago I wasn't *allowed* to go without you. Now, suddenly, you need an invitation."

Those eyes of his swept over her, heating all her secret places. "I want you to ask me. Do it."

"You realize I have no privacy in my life. Somehow, my family always knows whatever's going on with me whether I want them to know or not. And *you* can read my mind."

He put his napkin by his plate and stood. She gazed across at him looming over her. Beneath her irritation that he couldn't just accept her defeat on this without rubbing it in, she felt that special shiver. It was glorious, that shiver.

Even if what he'd said a minute ago about always being there to dry her tears were only pretty words, she knew he wanted her more than any man had ever wanted her before. More than she'd ever dared to hope any guy ever would.

It meant so much, the beautiful, intense, complete way he wanted her. It meant everything. She'd thought she was falling for him the day he told her he would enclose this patio for Wigs. But she hadn't known what falling was. Every day she fell deeper. There seemed no end to how far she could go. And with Jed, she wasn't afraid of her feelings. With Jed, she gloried in the fall.

Wigs, sitting near his feet, looked up at him expectantly. "Mrow?"

He glanced down at the cat. "It's only right that she asks me."

Wigs tipped his head to the side and replied thoughtfully, "Mrow."

And then Jed's eyes were on her again. "Well?"

She surrendered a lot more willingly than she would ever let him know. "Jed, will you please take me to my brother's wedding a week from Saturday?"

He wrapped those muscled arms across his wide chest and studied her for a moment that went on forever. "Come here."

Her heart did the happy dance inside her chest. "Will you or won't you?"

"Come here first. And when you get here, I want you to kiss me nice and slow."

Like there was any way she could resist an order like that. She rose and circled the table. Taking his face between her hands, she went on tiptoe to claim his lips, so soft and warm. His beard scruff scratched a little. It felt absolutely delicious.

He kept his arms across his chest. But slowly, he opened to her, let his tongue spar with hers. She did love the taste of him: smoky sweet from the barbecue sauce, with the added promise of any number of intimate delights to come.

When she dropped to her heels again, she asked, "Please?"

He uncrossed his arms at last and put a finger under her chin. "So we're understood about this, then? We are together and we're proud to be together and we don't give a good damn who knows it or what they think about it."

"That's easy for you to say. You never care what anyone else thinks."

"And neither should you. Are we understood?"

She gave in. Because he was right and because she adored the big lug. "Yes. We're understood. Will you go to the wedding with me?"

"Yes, Elise. I will." And then he whipped out an arm, hauled her good and close and kissed her until her knees gave way.

Carter Bravo and Paige Kettleman were married at six in the evening on the terrace at Belle Montagne Chateau ten miles outside of Justice Creek.

After the ceremony, they all moved inside for the reception, including a sit-down dinner for eighty. Paige and Carter had originally planned to use Bravo Catering for their reception. But then the business burned down. Elise had helped them find another caterer.

She'd assumed she would feel low on entering the banquet area and seeing the beautifully set tables, the floral centerpieces that Jody had designed. She'd just known that it would break her heart a little to watch the staff, in black slacks and vests and crisp white shirts, serving another caterer's menu.

But she didn't feel bad in the least. The dinner was beautifully done and Elise knew now that, thanks to Jed, she would have Bravo Catering up and running again, maybe even before the year was out.

So it wasn't a sad time at all. As it turned out, she was having a ball. Carter and Paige looked so happy and Quinn's speech as best man brought several big laughs and also a tear or two.

Jed was amazing. He looked so good in a gray silk

suit that hugged his wide shoulders perfectly and fit just right over his lean hips and muscular legs. He actually visited with people. He was friendly and seemed genuinely interested in what the older lady seated on his other side had to say.

Elise realized she'd never seen him in a social gathering before. She supposed she should have known he'd be capable of holding up his end at a party, should have realized it wasn't that he *couldn't* say all the right things and put people at ease. It was only that most of the time he just didn't bother. He was Jed Walsh and he made his own rules.

But tonight, he was charming. He joked around with Nell and went off to smoke a cigar with two of her brothers—and returned to the table looking completely relaxed.

She leaned close to him when he folded his big frame back into the chair beside her. "Did they threaten you in any way?"

"Get over it, Elise," he replied. "Your brothers are good guys. There were no threats. Not a one—and who's that blond guy over there, the one who keeps staring at you?"

The guy in question gave her a wincing sort of smile and a limp wave. "He's an old friend, that's all."

"Does your old friend have a name?"

Jed was so protective of her, she hesitated to tell him. But if he wanted to know, he would find out one way or another. Like Jack McCannon, Jed was always on the case. "His name is Biff."

"The dirtbag who borrowed money from you and then declared bankruptcy so he 'couldn't' pay you back?"

"He's been my friend since we were children."

"Some friend."

"Jed, he had a very tough time of it."

"Lots of people have a tough time of it."

"He's not a dirtbag."

"He is from where I'm sitting."

She whispered, "Keep your opinions to yourself, please. At least until we're alone—and I can't believe you remember who Biff is. I only mentioned him to you that one time."

"I remember everything you tell me." Across the room, Biff had started moving. "And the dirtbag is coming this way."

Oh, dear God. Jed was right, Biff was coming over. Did he have no instinct for self-preservation? "You let me handle this, Jed." Jed made a low snorting sound much too reminiscent of a bull about to charge. "I mean it," she warned. "If you can't say something nice, you'd better not say anything at all." She turned to Biff as he kept coming—which meant she couldn't see Jed. But she could sure feel his seething silence behind her.

"Elise." Biff, blond hair tousled, blue eyes full of regrets, stopped beside her chair. "It's so good to see you."

"Biff." She got up and gave him a quick hug and an air kiss, though she knew it wouldn't go over well with the snorting beast behind her. "How've you been?"

"Not good."

"I'm sorry to hear that—Biff, this is Jed. Jed Walsh, Biff Townley." She turned and blasted a giant, threatening smile at Jed.

Biff's hand came out. "So great to meet you. I heard you'd moved back to town. I love your books."

"Thanks." Jed had not risen. His face had that Mount

Rushmore look: carved in stone. He did give a nod, but made no move to take Biff's offered hand.

After several painful seconds, Biff gave it up and lowered his arm. "Ahem, Elise, I wonder if I might have a minute alone?"

"Of course," she said pleasantly. And then she turned to Jed again. "I'll be right back."

"All right." He spoke without inflection. Then he looked straight at Biff. "I'll be waiting." Somehow, he made that sound like a warning.

Biff actually flinched. "Er, great to meet you."

Jed didn't even nod that time.

Elise brushed Biff's arm. "Come on out to the terrace." She glanced back at Jed as she hustled Biff toward the wide steps that led outside. Jed was watching her walk away, his gaze brooding and dark.

"I think your boyfriend hates me," Biff said once they were out on the terrace beneath the tall trees.

Elise perched on the rock wall that defined the giant circular stone space. She was about to pretend Jed's reaction was nothing. But that seemed wrong, somehow. Biff *had* treated her shoddily and she'd never had the guts to confront him about it. Jed did have the guts.

And she was with Jed now. If he could tell the truth, well, so could she. "Jed is protective of me. I told him about the money I lent you that you never paid back."

Now Biff looked crushed. "I *couldn't* pay you back. You know that."

"No, Biff, I don't. Not really. Are you telling me that when you borrowed that eight thousand dollars from me, you actually believed you were going to repay it?"

Biff raked his fingers back through his hair. "Look, Elise. I just wanted to say that I've missed you, okay?

I miss hanging out now and then. I miss that I could always count on you, on your level head and good advice, on the great dinners you would cook to make me feel better when my life was going all to hell."

Elise carefully smoothed her silk skirt. "You didn't answer my question."

"Well, I—I *wanted* to pay you back. Of course I did."

"When *will* you pay me back, Biff?"

He stared off toward a granite peak far in the distance. "Seriously? You want to get into this now, at your brother's wedding?"

"No time is a good time when you don't pay your debts." From where she sat, she could see the archway to the banquet room. Jed came through it. She met those green eyes and gave a slight shake of her head. He took her cue that she didn't need him—not yet, anyway. Moving to a tree-shaded spot on the outer edge of the archway, he waited.

And she knew why. Because she was his woman and he took care of what was his.

Her heart seemed to expand in her chest and great tenderness flooded her. Elise had known she was falling for him, and that she kept falling deeper. But it was not until that moment, when he came out on the terrace just in case she might need him, that she realized she had fallen all the way.

She loved Jed Walsh.

Chapter Nine

"I didn't come out here to be insulted," Biff huffed.

Elise hardly heard him. She was much too busy dealing with what had just happened in her heart.

I love him. I love Jed.

It was real. It was true. It was the most beautiful thing that had ever happened to her.

"Did you hear a word I just said?" Biff demanded.

"Not really." Elise kept her eyes on the big man standing in the sun-dappled shadows by the door to the banquet room. "I don't think we have much more to say to each other as of now, Biff. You have my cell number. Come up with a payment plan and give me a call."

"But I just *told* you—"

"You take care now." With a wave of her hand, she dismissed him. As she started toward Jed, he left his spot by the door and came for her. They met in the middle of the terrace. She needed to touch him, so she reached up and smoothed the lapel of his jacket.

He caught her hand. "I hope you put the dirtbag in his place."

"I think I did. More or less." She gave a half shrug. Biff Townley hardly mattered, not when every fiber of her being was vibrating with sheer happiness. Music had started up in the banquet room. "Will you dance with me, Jed?"

He kissed the tops of her knuckles and her heart felt bigger, her knees weaker in the sweetest sort of way. "Never was much of a dancer."

"Does that mean yes or no?"

"You want to dance with me, you got it." He wrapped her hand around his arm and led her back beneath the archway to where the music played.

That night, she told him she loved him—or rather, she shouted it good and loud as he pulsed inside her. A little later, when he turned off the lamp, held her close and stroked her hair, she wondered if it could be possible that he hadn't really noticed her yelling, "Oh, Jed, I love you!" minutes before.

He didn't say anything about it.

And she didn't ask. Let him chalk it up to one of those things a woman says in the heat of passion. She did love him, yes. With all of her heart. But she wasn't really ready to talk about what that might mean yet.

Monday morning, just as they were sitting down to a breakfast of poached eggs, toast and cantaloupe wedges, Jed's publicist called.

"It's official. A week from Friday, I'm on *NY at Night*,"

Jed said when he hung up the phone. "We'll fly in Thursday, returning Sunday."

Elise kind of wondered if she'd heard him right. "You're serious? You're going to meet Drew Golden and be on *NY at Night*?"

Wearing a look of great boredom, he sipped his coffee. "Isn't that what I just said? And it's damned inconvenient if you ask me. I hate a break in my rhythm when things are moving right along."

She chuckled at that. "You hate a break in your rhythm anytime and you know it."

"True. But it's a big freaking deal to get a spot on Golden's show, just ask my agent."

"Well, I have to say that *I'm* thoroughly impressed."

He drank more coffee, watching her face as he sipped and swallowed, his eyes low and lazy. "Hmm. I like you impressed, all pink-cheeked and adoring."

She spread jam on her toast. "*Adoring* might be carrying it a bit far."

"Maybe I should take you back to bed. You can show me just how impressed you are with me and my many accomplishments."

Okay, the plain fact was she did adore him and she would love nothing so much as to go straight back to bed with him. But then again, it was a lot of fun to give him a bad time. "I never said I was impressed with *you*, exactly."

He ate some cantaloupe. "But you are. Thoroughly. I'm an impressive guy."

"Egotistical much? And what's this *we*? I take it you think that I'm going with you to New York."

"Because you *are* going with me."

She was thrilled that she was going and she loved him more than life itself. But sometimes he needed reminding that he didn't actually rule the world. "I don't recall your inviting me."

"Ah. You need a special invitation, do you?"

"Yes, I do. Remember Carter's wedding?"

"As though I could forget. It was two days ago."

"I'm referring to how you insisted that I had to ask you to go with me."

"That was only right."

"Well then you should have no problem understanding how I might want you to ask me if would like to go to New York with you."

"You're my assistant. It's your job to be where I need you." He said it in that low, rough voice that sent little flares of excitement pulsing in her most secret places.

Still, she didn't give in. "So you're planning to write while you're there?"

"I just might."

"But you said we would be flying back on Sunday and Sunday is my day off."

He frowned. "Wait a minute. Are you saying that you really don't want to go?" He looked marginally worried.

And her heart melted. "Let me lay it out for you. I'm giving you grief because you just assumed I would do whatever you wanted me to."

"But you *are* coming with me?"

For such a brilliant man, he could be dense as a post. She said nothing, just gave him a moment to figure it out.

Finally, he did. "Elise."

"Yes, Jed?"

"Will you please go with me to New York next week?"

"Why, Jed. How lovely of you to ask. I would be delighted to go."

For that, she got one of his rare half smiles. "Excellent—and I still think I need to take you back to bed."

"What for?"

He set down his spoon, pushed back his chair and came for her, scooping her up in his arms the way he loved to do. "Come on upstairs. I'll show you."

And he did, to their mutual delight.

A week and a half later, they left Wigs in Deirdre's care and flew first class to JFK.

Elise tipped her roomy seat back, accepted a glass of champagne and sipped it slowly. "I haven't flown first class in forever."

Jed looked up from texting his social media assistant. "Ever been to New York?"

She had another sip of delicious bubbly. "Twice. Both times first class, too. When I was eighteen, my great aunt Agnes took Tracy and me to shop for our senior-ball dresses. Aunt Agnes always flies first class. Then in college, Tracy and I got one of those package deals—hotel, dinners at a couple of nice restaurants, two Broadway shows and first-class flights. That was a great trip. We walked all over Manhattan."

He watched her in that special way he had that made her feel wanted and understood and totally fascinating. "How long's it been since you've seen Tracy?"

"Not since mid-May, when she left for Seattle."

"When will she come back to Justice Creek again?"

"She'll be home for Thanksgiving—at least that's the plan as of now. But you never know. She's mentioned a guy she likes. If that goes somewhere she may want to be with him for the holiday."

"You miss her."

"Yeah. But it's not as bad as it used to be." *Not since I fell for you—and kept on falling. Right into love.* "She's happy and I'm happy for her."

He tipped his head to the side, studying her. "So you're not secretly longing to hop a flight to Seattle?"

"No. I meant what I told you weeks ago. Tracy and I had years together. Great years. She'll always be a sister to me and we both know we can count on each other if things get too rough. But our lives have gone in different directions now and I'm good with that."

His gaze never left her face. "So are you saying that *you're* happy now?"

She leaned across the wide armrest to slip her arm through his. "Very. And I have a lot to be happy about. Thanks to you, my bank account is no longer on life support. The future looks bright in a number of ways. Plus, here I am on a first-class fight to New York—with you, which is the best part of all."

He leaned even closer and whispered in her ear, "You never know. You might decide to stay with me when the book's done, after all."

The way she felt right now, she never wanted to be anywhere else. But something in his expression had her wondering if he imagined she might remain his assistant, too.

Then again, no. She'd made it more than clear that this one book was the only one she would type for him.

So instead of reminding him of their original agreement, she whispered teasingly, "Stay with you? You'd better watch out. I just might never leave."

He had that look then, the one that melted her panties. "I was hoping you would say that."

And then he kissed her, slow and sweet.

* * *

They had a suite at the Knickerbocker right on Times Square, but with a beautiful view of Bryant Park. The rooms were all cool grays and misty blues. Very soothing. And the bathtub was waiting.

Yes, they got a little bit distracted and spent more time than they probably should have enjoying that tub together and also the very comfy king-size bed. Elise had to hustle to be ready in time to meet Jed's agent and editor for dinner. She'd brought a little black dress to wear and breathed a sigh of relief when the dress fit pretty well. True, it was snug where it had once flowed loosely over her waist and hips. And about her cleavage? She had a whole bunch more of that than before. It was kind of spilling out a little.

She turned to ask Jed if the dress made her look fat. One look in those smoldering jade eyes and she knew that if she *did* look fat, it totally worked for Jed. She faced the mirror again and grinned at her reflection. The dress would definitely do.

"Beautiful," he said in that gruff tone that told her he wouldn't mind getting that dress right off her again. He started toward her. She could see him coming over her shoulder.

She showed him the hand in the mirror. "Don't even think it. We have to go."

Jed's agent, his editor and a vice president from his publishing house were all waiting at their table when they entered the restaurant. The host seated Elise next to Jed, with his agent, Holly Prescott, on her other side.

Elise had a good time with Holly. The agent, who dressed like a fashion model and weighed maybe ninety pounds soaking wet, was a little like Jed—gruff and direct, smart and funny.

The men carried on their own conversation as Holly peppered Elise with questions on everything from her family and her previous occupations to how she liked working with Jed. Elise told the other woman that she was a caterer by profession. She said that she and Jed worked great together, but typing for a living wasn't her idea of a good time. "Which is why I only agreed to be his assistant for this one book."

Holly frowned. "But given that you two work so well together, maybe you'll reconsider, change your mind and stay on with him…"

Elise answered honestly. "No way. It's a great experience, working for Jed, and I'm enjoying it. But it's not forever. I'm not spending my life at a desk. Working for Jed now is going to make it possible for me to reopen my catering business, hopefully soon after this book's done."

In the meantime, she heard the vice president, Dan Short, describing Jed's bright future with his publisher. Carl Burgess, Jed's editor, got all excited when he heard that Jed was two thirds through the rough draft of the new book, which had the working title *McCannon's Fall*.

"So it's going well at last," Carl said with clear relief.

And Jed gave a dry chuckle. "Don't jinx me, Carl." He turned to Elise. "But yeah," he said, his eyes only for her at that moment. "I'm back on track and it feels really good."

Jed seemed happy and relaxed when they all walked out together after the long meal was through. Carl and the vice president hailed cabs and left. Holly said she needed a quick chat with Jed—nothing major but it would take a few minutes. At Jed's suggestion, Elise went back inside and ordered an Irish coffee at the cozy bar in the front of the restaurant.

From her corner stool, she could see Jed and Holly with their heads together standing under an awning not far from the entrance. Really, she had no clue what could have come up that Holly just had to share with Jed immediately...

Jed had been listening to Holly talk without really saying anything for close to ten minutes when he decided he needed to cut through the yadda-yadda and get back to Elise. "Stop trying to be subtle, Holly. It's not your style."

"Well, I hate to overstep my bounds, that's all."

"Oh, come on. When has a boundary ever slowed you down before?"

Holly narrowed her sharp eyes at him. "Don't be an ass. It pisses me off."

He let out a bark of laughter. "That's more like it. What's on your mind?"

"It's Elise."

His gut tightened. "On second thought, watch your mouth."

Holly raised a placating hand. "Stop. I like her. Carl and Dan liked her. And I can tell you like her, too—a lot more than you've ever liked anyone, if you ask me."

"Yes, I do. Get to the point."

"You're together, right? And I don't just mean during working hours."

"We are absolutely together. And we're staying that way."

"Which is great. I've never seen you this happy or this relaxed. And being happy and relaxed clearly works for you. Suddenly you're flying through the book you got nowhere on for a year."

"Whatever you're getting at, you're not there yet."

"Fine. Elise told me she's going back to catering as soon as you've finished the manuscript."

That had him falling back a step. "What did you say?"

"I said, Elise told me—"

"Never mind. I heard you." Okay, he knew Elise wasn't solid yet on continuing as his assistant. But on the plane, she'd said she was thinking about it. Didn't she? "*When* did she tell you she was going back to catering?"

"While Dan Short was describing all the big things they're going to be doing for you when *McCannon's Fall* comes out."

Crap.

How could he not have known this? How could he have read her so wrong when he could tell just by watching her face what she was thinking? He'd been so certain that he was making progress with her, that she was slowly realizing she wanted to stay.

Because she *had* to stay. Now that he'd found her, there was no way he could lose her. He'd never find another assistant like her.

She left even Anna in the dust. And it wasn't only her ability to type while he shouted and threw things. Elise had great instincts when it came to the story, to the characters. Yeah, he got advice and feedback on the books from Carl and Holly, from his virtual assistant and a number of copy editors and beta readers. But he'd never had anyone to bounce things off of day-to-day before. He didn't give his trust easily; critique groups and writing buddies weren't for him.

If he lost Elise...

But he wouldn't.

The woman loved him. He saw it when he looked in those dark eyes of hers. She'd even said it in bed the night of her brother's wedding. True, she'd been having an orgasm at the time. But he knew that she'd meant it by the nervous glances she'd sent him later, by the way she'd watched him the next morning at breakfast, shy and sweet. Hopeful, but not really ready to talk about it yet—or at least, that was how he'd read her signals that morning.

Had he read her all wrong about loving him, too?

He didn't think so. She cared for him. He knew she did. And she wanted to stay with him.

Now he just had to make her see that she should stay with him professionally as well as personally. He needed to get her to admit that there was no way throwing parties for strangers could beat what he had to offer her, financially speaking. And creatively, too.

"I just thought I ought to let you know," said Holly.

"Thanks."

"You've still got time to change her mind."

"Yes, I do."

"And, hey. Think of it this way. If it doesn't work out, you were looking for an assistant when you found her."

For that, Holly got his deadliest stare. "She's not going back to catering, don't worry."

Holly let out a slow breath. "Well, good. Because frankly, we've already learned the hard way that there aren't a whole lot of assistants who have what it takes to type your books for you."

Chapter Ten

When Jed slid onto the bar stool beside her, Elise leaned into his solid strength. Loving him was a revelation to her. All he had to do was move in close and the world got warmer and brighter.

She asked, "Everything all right with Holly?"

He wrapped an arm around her and pressed a kiss to her temple. "Fine. She had some suggestions for the interview tomorrow—how's the Irish coffee?"

"Delicious."

"Want another?"

When she shook her head, he grabbed her hand and pulled her out into the slightly sticky warmth of the August night.

It was a little after ten. They strolled around Times Square for a while. Elise enjoyed the lights and hurrying crowds.

But she liked it even more when he took her back to

the hotel, peeled off her tight black dress and showed her how glad he was that she'd come to New York with him.

The next day, they had room service for breakfast. Jed had a visit to his publisher's offices at eleven, followed by a working lunch with Holly, the publicity team and more publishing executives, so Elise had several hours on her own.

She spent some "me" time in the hotel spa, had a room-service lunch and then took a cab to Bloomingdale's, where she spent more of her recently hard-earned cash than she probably should have on a new flared skirt, silk top and sexy high-heeled shoes to wear to the *NY at Night* taping at five.

A limo took her to the studio, where she was ushered to a great seat on the aisle in the third row. Jed had the first guest slot after Drew Golden's monologue.

And Jed was good. Really good. He seemed totally relaxed, joking with Drew Golden as though the two of them were BFFs from birth. After a quick synopsis of Jed's personal history, from growing up as the only son of a bona fide survivalist, to a little about his years in the service, they talked about the first Jack McCannon book and how each one had sold better than the last.

Jed leaned back in his chair with one ankle hitched across his other knee and joked about the ways to kill people. "Because I have to tell you, Drew. Jack McCannon knows them all."

They talked about the potential for a series of Mc-Cannon movies. Jed said that he and his team were working on that. And then Golden had questions about the development of the McCannon character through the books so far, about what would change in Jack's life going forward.

Jed said, "Jack will be meeting a woman he can't walk away from, a woman who changes the direction of his life."

Drew Golden chuckled. "Is it possible that life is paralleling fiction here?"

Jed put it right out there. "Absolutely."

"Can you tell us about her?"

"Only that she's brilliant and beautiful, that nothing gets past her and I don't know how I ever got along without her. I even like her damn cat. And I hate cats."

That got a laugh and also a round of enthusiastic applause.

Blushing, Elise clapped, too. She felt like the heroine of her own personal romantic movie. Jed not only cared about her, but he was also willing to say so in front of a nationwide audience.

After the show, a production assistant came and led her backstage, where Jed was waiting. He put his arm around her and nuzzled her hair. "God, you're gorgeous."

She confessed, "I spent way too much money in Bloomingdale's."

He pulled her closer and whispered, "I like your new clothes, but I like what's under them even better."

She shook a finger at him. "Later for that." And then she smoothed the collar of his sport coat, feeling tender and fond and so very proud of him. "It went so well. You were really good."

"Did I say too much?" He sounded almost hesitant.

And she was blushing all over again. "Not too much. No way." She put a hand to her heart. "I'm keeping those words you said right here, storing them up, you know? To remember for all of my life." And then she couldn't resist a little teasing. "Especially the part about how you actually like Wigs."

He introduced her to the publicist and one of the *NY at Night* producers. Feeling dazed and happy and out of her element, but not really in a bad way, she smiled and said how great it was to meet them.

Finally, Jed took her out through a door backstage. The guy from the publicity department went with them, but then flagged down a cab and left.

Elise watched him go. "So…dinner with more publishing people?"

He shook his head. "Tonight and tomorrow, it's just you and me."

As it turned out, Jed didn't write a single word that weekend. He wanted a little time apart with Elise and he took it.

They had dinner that night at his favorite café in the Village. And Saturday, they visited the Arms and Armor collection at the Met, took the subway to the best pizzeria in Bedford-Stuyvesant and had dinner in a rooftop garden, the guests of a writer friend of his in Queens.

Saturday night, he kept her up very late. He couldn't get enough of her, really. Sexually, she managed to be shy and adventurous, funny and alluring all at the same time. They made love on just about every available surface in the hotel suite and when she finally fell asleep in his arms, he brushed the tangled hair off her forehead and tried to decide how to deal with what Holly had told him.

He still had two months until his deadline. Should

he bring it up now, ask Elise to reconsider their original agreement, to think about what would sweeten the pot enough to make her give up on the damn catering thing and stay on with him? Or should he play it out to the end and knock her socks off with some kind of terrific, irresistible offer she couldn't refuse? Whatever the hell that might be...

On the flight home to Justice Creek, he was still trying to decide which way to go.

Elise noticed. Which shouldn't have surprised him. It was one of the many things he loved about her. Nothing got by her for long.

He was staring off toward the door to the cockpit, endlessly considering his limited options, when she asked if something was bothering him.

It was a good opening. But he wasn't ready to make his move yet—mainly because he hadn't decided what that move should be. "Just working through a few plot points."

"I'm here if you need to talk about it."

I'm here...

Exactly. And she needed to stay here. With him, in every way. If only he could figure out how to make her see that.

The Thursday following the New York trip, when Elise checked her phone right after lunch, she found a text from Biff Townley.

I thought about what you said, Elise. And you were right. I have your money. Where should I send the check?

She didn't know whether to be pleased that he was finally coming through, angry that she'd had to tell him off to get him to pay up...or worried that maybe he couldn't really afford to give her the money back.

Pleased, she decided. Biff had borrowed that money over a year ago and he'd promised to return it to her within a month or two. It wasn't her problem how he'd finally come up with it.

So she texted back a thank-you and Jed's address. She'd had most of her bills and correspondence rerouted here. That way she didn't have to stop by her apartment every Sunday before making a run to the bank or whatever.

Plus, the way things were going between her and Jed now, she might never move back. She grinned like a fool at the thought.

Her phone beeped. Another text from Biff: I saw your boyfriend on NY at Night. The guy's really gone on you, huh?

I'm gone on him, too, so it's working out great.

They say he's a little bit crazy.

Elise scowled at the phone. Biff was way more annoying than she'd ever realized before. She replied, Yeah. In a very good way.

Ha, ha. I get why he's gone on you. You looked amazing at the wedding. Sexy. That bit of total squickiness was followed by a heart-eyes emoji that had Elise full-out gaping at her phone.

Biff Townley texting a move on her? That was just wrong.

What are you up to, Biff?

I told you at the wedding. I miss you. Meet me for coffee? It's been too long since we really talked.

Did you somehow not get that I'm with Jed now?

What? He doesn't let you see your old friends?

Where was this going? No place good. She texted back a final That was uncalled-for. You have the address. Send the check. Goodbye, Biff.

She hit Send and tossed the phone on the bed. If he came back with one more word of douche-baggery, she would block him and good riddance—even if he never gave her money back.

"Trust me?" Jack tried a reassuring smile. Sadika only stared at him, her incomparable face far too composed. "We have no choice. We have to jump."

Did she understand? Did she even hear him? He held those dazed eyes of hers for a count of five that they really couldn't afford. K's men were coming.

"No choice," he repeated, not happy with their chances. The river below ran cold and swift, ready to suck them under. But K's men would not be gentle, either. He wrapped her arms around his neck, lifted her and guided those long legs around his waist. "Hold on good and tight. Do not let go."

"Okay, what's the matter?" Jed watched Elise type the question and realized he'd failed to give the signal to stop. "Elise." Her fingers stopped moving. She assumed her waiting pose. It was a thing of beauty—her hands poised, shoulders relaxed. "We're taking a break."

She glanced up at him then. "Why? I think it's fine. Moving right along. What's not working for you?"

He looked down at her sweet upturned face. "It's you."

"Huh?"

"Something's bugging you. What?"

She gave him an eye roll and gestured at the screen. "Take a look. I don't think I missed a word you said."

"I know you didn't. You never do. But you were biting your lip. You even wrinkled your nose."

She laughed. "Wrinkled my nose?" She pressed her hand to her chest and faked a gasp. "No wonder you stopped me."

"You're trying really hard to blow me off. It's not working. Talk."

"Jed…" The woman could put a world of exasperation into the three little letters that made up his name.

"Come on." He held down his hand.

She eyed it warily. "Where?"

"Out to the catio. The sun is shining and your damn cat is always happy to see you." She laid her fingers in his and he pulled her up from the chair.

Outside, they sat on the sofa with the cat stretched out and purring on Elise's other side. She petted the big creature in long strokes, from his head to his tail. A smile curved her lips, but her eyes were far away.

"I'm waiting," he said.

Elise sagged back against the cushions. She *had* been distracted back there in the office. She kept thinking what a complete jerk Biff was.

And she'd kind of decided not to mention the texts to Jed. After all, she'd handled Biff. And Jed really was kind of a caveman. She had no idea how he'd react when he heard that Biff had put a move on her, even if it was only via text.

Jed hooked his big arm around her and pulled her closer. She settled her head on his shoulder. "Talk, Elise."

She gave in and told him. "I had a text from Biff Townley when I checked my phone at lunchtime."

Jed pressed his lips against her hair. "And?"

"He asked for an address so he could send me a check."

"So that's good news, then."

She sighed. "Yeah."

"Which doesn't explain why you were wrinkling your nose during the bridge scene."

"He pissed me off, okay?"

"How?"

She glanced up at Jed again. He was being wonderful and she was making him work for every smallest bit of information. She made up her mind. "Wait right here. I'll get my phone and show you."

He let her go without comment.

When she came back outside, Wigs was snuggled up close to him, purring louder than before.

She stopped at the sofa but she didn't sit down. "I'm going to show you these texts and you're *not* going to do anything about them."

He stared up at her, simultaneously lazy and predatory, the way Wigs sometimes watched the birds beyond the patio. If Jed had a tail, it would be twitching.

She added, "I've already handled the situation. There really is nothing for you to do."

He held out his hand. "Just give me the phone, Elise."

She dropped down next to him on the side Wigs wasn't already occupying, punched up the conversation in question and handed it over. He read it through quickly and passed the phone back to her.

"Well?" she demanded.

"The guy's a dirtball. It's not news—and you're right. You handled it. I promise not to hunt him down and punch his lights out. If I happen to run into him on the street, though, all bets are off."

"Thank you. I think."

He hooked his arm around her neck and drew her close to him again, pressing his nose to her cheek, breathing in, scenting her. "He's not worth biting your lip over."

"You don't get it."

"So explain it to me."

"I thought he was a basically good guy, okay? I used to consider him a dear friend. I would cook beautiful dinners for him and listen to him go on and on about how awful his wife was. And I would sympathize and top off his wineglass. Like *she* was the problem. I didn't even know Biff's wife, really, and I said a lot of bad things about her, and now I have to face the fact that she's probably the one I should have been feeling sorry for. I had my head up my ass for years, you know? And every time I have to face more evidence of my own past idiocy, it makes me want to scream."

He tightened his arm around her neck, pulling her close again so he could touch his warm lips to her ear.

His beard scruff tickled in the loveliest way. "Go ahead. Scream."

She elbowed him in the side. "Next you'll be giving me knives to throw."

"For that, there would have to be training." His low voice sent hot shivers racing across the surface of her skin. "That could be interesting, training you."

"Training me." She turned her head and kissed him, just a quick one, because she couldn't resist. "You make that sound really dirty."

He moved then, turning and rising in one seamless motion, his hand sliding down her arm to capture her wrist.

With a squeak of surprise, she found herself slung over his shoulder, blinking down at the patio stones. She hit him on the hard curve of his perfect butt because it was in easy range.

He grunted. "Do that again."

"I just might. And I shouldn't have to remind you that we have a page goal to meet."

"And we will. But first, I need to show you something up in my room."

"Let me guess. Your bed."

He didn't even bother to answer, just banded his arm around her dangling legs and headed for the French doors.

They met Deirdre on the way up the stairs. Elise realized she wasn't the least concerned that the housekeeper had finally witnessed the sight of Jed carrying her off to his lair.

Because, well, why shouldn't he carry her up to his room? She loved him and she was pretty sure he loved her, too, even if they hadn't actually talked about that yet. And come on, she *slept* in Jed's room. Deirdre had to have figured that out by now, anyway.

Bottom line: Elise was in love with the boss and she didn't care who knew it. She gave Deirdre a wave as they passed her. Deirdre grinned, nodded and continued down.

The next day, Elise got a letter and a big check in the mail. The envelope was creased, smudged and forwarded from her burned-down apartment on Central Street.

It wasn't from Biff. It was from her long-gone, struggling-artist ex-boyfriend, Sean. When she opened the envelope, she found a two-page handwritten letter and a check for twenty thousand dollars inside.

Her hands shaking only a little, she read,

Dear Elise,
I'm guessing you never expected to hear from me again—let alone for me to do the right thing and return the money you so generously invested in me. The hard truth is, I never planned to contact you again and I certainly never intended to give you back your money.

But it's been a long road for me. I have learned much about what's right and what isn't. And I have met someone special. Her name is Fiona. Fiona says that to walk in peace with the universe and realize my full potential as an artist, I must find a way to right every wrong I have perpetrated.

And let me tell you, Elise. That is a tall order…

A laugh burst from Elise right then. She was standing at the little built-in desk just off the kitchen area where Deirdre always left the mail. "Jed!" she called, and headed for the office where he'd remained while she'd walked the main floor during one of her five-minute breaks.

She found him leaning over her desk, studying the manuscript file she'd left open when she got up for her walk.

He rose to his height when she entered and she waved the check at him. "I just got a check for twenty thousand dollars and a letter from my ex-boyfriend, Sean. You have to read this…" Laughing, she went to him and held up the letter so they could read it together.

"Sean is a real piece of work," he said once they'd both reached the end.

"I sure knew how to pick 'em, didn't I?"

He sent her a wry glance. "At least you used the past tense when you said that."

"Of course I did. Because present company is definitely excluded—in fact, I think you must bring me good luck. If this check doesn't bounce, I've got my money back from Sean. And what I lent Biff is supposedly in the mail." She waved the letter. "Did you read the part where Sean says Fiona gave him the money to send to me?"

"Yeah, I noticed that."

She held up the check again. The account was in Sean's name and the signature was Sean's. "I really hope Fiona knows what she's doing. I kind of feel sorry for her."

"Don't." It was a command.

"But—"

"I mean it, Elise. He owes you the money. How he got

it to give it back to you isn't your problem. Plus, he says right in that letter that Fiona is 'a very wealthy woman.'"

"Right." She read from the letter. "'Fiona is a very wealthy woman and she's offered to support my art and help me get solid with the universe.'"

"Translation—Fiona is supporting him and also paying his debts, which is Fiona's choice, Elise, and not—"

"—my problem. I know, I heard you the first time." She thought it over a little more and then shrugged. "So okay, then. Fiona's on her own with Sean. Sunday, I'll put this check in the bank and in a week to ten days, I'll know if it's good or not."

He tipped up her chin and kissed the end of her nose. "That's my girl."

Saturday, the check from Biff arrived. And Sunday, Elise stopped off at the bank and deposited both checks.

After the bank, she went to her sister-in-law Addie's baby shower at Clara's house. Addie Kenwright Bravo had married Elise's brother James just last March. At the time of the wedding, Addie was already pregnant with the baby of her best friend, Brandon Hall, through artificial insemination. Brandon had died of cancer at the end of January. So technically, James was not the baby's father. But everyone in the Bravo family knew that James loved that unborn child as his own.

And they all loved Addie. She was small and spunky, independent and big-hearted, and today she was wearing a yellow dress printed with daisies. She looked like a walking ray of sunshine—or maybe a waddling one. A month from her due date, Addie seemed ready to pop.

They played baby-shower games: "baby sketch artist," "baby items in a bag" and "don't say baby." There was lunch and cake and champagne for anyone who wanted it. Addie opened a huge pile of baby gifts.

Later, Jody pulled Elise into a free corner of the kitchen and asked how she was doing.

"Terrific," Elise replied with enthusiasm. "Jed's an amazing guy and I'm happy, Jody. Really happy. I almost can't believe it. Two and a half months ago, my world was a total disaster. My love life was nonexistent, just like my bank balance. Now I have money in the bank and the greatest guy in the world thinks I'm the hottest thing around."

Jody beamed. "I saw you two at the wedding. Anyone could see he's crazy about you."

"It's mutual, believe me."

"You do have that glow."

"And I can't thank you and Clara enough. You put me to work, kept me busy and focused and made sure I didn't starve during the worst of it. And Nell... Don't tell her I said so. She thinks she knows everything. But I owe her large."

Jody put up a hand like a witness swearing an oath. "I will never say a word to her."

Elise laughed. "Whew."

"So, you'll be staying on as Jed's assistant, then?"

"God, no. I hate typing."

"But you're so good at it and Jed pays big money, right?"

"Money isn't everything—and yeah, it's easy for me to say, now I'm no longer destitute. I also happen to mean it. I am not typing one more word than I absolutely have to. Why doesn't anyone seem to understand that just because a person's good at something doesn't mean they're dying to spend their life doing it? As soon as this book is done, so am I." She lowered her voice to a confidential whisper. "But if it all works out the way I'm hoping, I *will* be staying on with Jed."

Jody's smile was soft. "I love seeing you happy. And it's about time." She held up her empty champagne flute. "Don't move. I'm filling up my glass and then I have something to propose to you."

Right on cue, Clara stepped up with a tray of full ones. "More champagne, little sister?"

"You're a lifesaver." Jody switched out her empty flute for a full one and they chatted with Clara for a few minutes—about how great the party was, and how big Clara's one-year-old, Kiera, had grown.

Then Clara moved off to share the bubbly with her other guests and Elise picked up her conversation with Jody where they'd left off. "What kind of proposal?"

"First, are you still thinking of opening Bravo Catering again?"

"I *am* opening Bravo Catering again. That was always the plan. It was just that for a few really bleak months there I had no clue how I would ever make it happen."

"Would you consider maybe going into partnership with me?"

Elise got the loveliest rising feeling in her chest. "Bloom and Bravo Catering, together?"

"Well, I mean before the fire, we did several weddings together, right? That went so well. And I liked working with you when you were filling in at Bloom, too. I think we make a great team. So I was wondering, what if we formally combined forces? We could still keep both companies, and look for a new, larger location, a shop where we would each have our own store, but adjoining, you know? Two separate entrances, one for Bravo Catering and one for Bloom, but we would design the space so the two shops kind of flow together. Food and flowers. I think it could be great."

Elise waved her hand in front of her face. "Jody. I think I'm going to cry."

"Good tears?"

"The best kind." Elise grabbed her sister and gave her a hug.

Jody hugged her right back, then took her by the shoulders to look in her eyes. "So you'll consider it?"

"Consider it? I love it. I'm in. And I'll have the money for it, no problem, thanks to Jed. But I'm working with him dawn to dusk on the book until he finishes the manuscript. I only have Sundays off and I need at least one day a week to run errands and decompress a little."

"I know. I get that."

"He's ahead of schedule, so maybe he'll be done early—sometime in October, if we get lucky. His deadline, though, is November first. I can't commit to anything until then. But I promise, Jody, from the first of November, I'm your partner."

Jody squealed in delight—and then clapped her hand over her mouth and shook her head, blushing. "Okay. I'm excited. Tell me, does it show?"

"Me, too. I really wasn't looking forward to being completely on my own."

"I know. I always envied you and Tracy, to have each other to count on. Now, *we'll* have each other. I'm so thrilled you said yes."

Elise got back home at a little after five.

She found Jed out on the catio with Wigs. "How are my guys?"

Jed patted the spot beside him on the sofa. She took it. He wrapped an arm around her and she snuggled close, resting her head on the hard bulge of his shoulder. He rubbed his scruffy chin against her hair and asked, "So how was Addie's baby shower?"

"You would have loved it," she teased.

A low, disbelieving sound rumbled up from his big chest. "Did you play those silly girly games—'pin the tail on the baby'? 'Bobbing for nipples'?"

"How do you even *know* about baby-shower games?"

"I'm a writer. I have to know a little bit about everything—plus, I went to a coed shower once, back when I was married to Carrie. The experience was one I would prefer never to repeat."

"Oh, you poor man." She patted his cheek.

"You need to kiss me and make it all better, wipe the memory of that terrible time from my conscious mind."

"I'm on it." And she kissed him, slowly and with a lot of tongue. "How's that?"

"I think I *might* be all right now."

"I'm so glad."

"But maybe you should kiss me once more, just to be sure."

With a happy laugh, she cradled his face and pressed her lips to his. When she lifted away, he tried to grab her close again. But she could not wait another minute to tell him about her conversation with Jody. She pushed at his chest. "I have news."

"About…?"

"I had a long talk with Jody."

He grinned. "You should see your face. Apparently, Jody had something really good to tell you."

"She did. She had an offer for me."

His arms loosened around her. "What kind of offer?"

She sat back against the cushions. "It's like this. As soon as the book is done, Jody and I are going into partnership together. We'll get a new space and combine her flower shop with my catering business." She kicked off her sandals and drew her legs up yoga-style. "It's a stroke of genius, perfect for both of us." A gleeful little laugh escaped her. "Jody suggested it and, well, I couldn't say yes fast enough. Not only will we do weddings together the way we were doing before I had to close down, we each get foot traffic from the other.

"I'm thinking I'll have a bakery area—great coffee and pastries, you know? I'll be open the same hours as Bloom. People come in to buy flowers and they can get a coffee and a muffin. Or they come for coffee and get tempted by Bloom. I can't wait to..." Her voice trailed off as the expression on his face finally registered.

He didn't look the least bit pleased to be hearing all this.

Chapter Eleven

You're not going into business with your sister, Jed thought but somehow had the presence of mind not to say. *I need you right here, working for me.*

This was bad. He should have had this out with her before she managed to go off and make a deal with Jody. But he'd thought he had more time—weeks yet—to create a workable plan, to come up with an offer so tempting she'd realize there was no way she could refuse.

What offer is that, exactly? mocked a knowing voice in his mind. *And what if she still refuses, no matter what you offer her?*

She'd never given him the slightest indication that she might change her mind and continue as his assistant after the book was done—except for that time on the plane to New York. But then he'd only *thought* she might stay on; he'd heard what he wanted to hear. She'd meant she would stay with *him*, not that she would keep typing his books.

And if he was any other man he would be telling himself he had to learn to accept her position on this.

But he wasn't just any guy. He had a certain process that worked for him and she was a big part of that process. She was not a cog in a wheel, easily replaceable.

Without her, the damn wheel didn't turn.

Well, you are going to need to replace her. Get over it and move on. The voice of reason in his head was calm. Logical. Right.

And he refused to listen to it.

That year after Anna left had been pure hell. He needed to find a way *not* to go through that again.

And if there was no way, if she was leaving no matter what once he finished *McCannon's Fall*, he damn well didn't want to know that now.

Now, the book had to come first. Having to accept her leaving would only mess with his mind and slow down his writing. That couldn't happen.

He would get to the end of the damn book and then find a way to convince Elise to keep working with him—so what if she had plans to work with her sister? Plans change.

And she was looking at him strangely now. "Jed. What is it?" She put her soft hand on his. "What's wrong?"

He ordered his expression to relax, even managed to form what for him passed as a smile. "Not a thing."

"But you seemed so—"

"There's nothing," he lied, turning his hand over, clasping her fingers, giving them a reassuring squeeze. "So. You and Jody, huh?"

She looked so serious now—because she knew him

better than anyone ever had before. She knew exactly what was bothering him, which her next words made painfully clear. "You said the day you hired me that if it worked out with me, you weren't going to like it when I left. I get that, I do. And I don't want to leave *you*—it's just the job. Long-term, it's not for me."

"I understand. Don't worry. Everything's fine."

She wanted badly to believe him. He could see it in those big dark eyes of hers. "You're sure?"

"Of course."

Elise *didn't* believe him.

He definitely had something on his mind that he wasn't sharing. But she'd asked and encouraged—and then prodded him for good measure. He didn't want to get into it, whatever it was.

Well, okay. She would leave it alone until he was ready to talk about it.

They went inside, had some dinner and watched a movie in the media room downstairs. He took her to bed and made smoking hot love to her.

That week, the book moved along at lightning speed. Jed was really on a roll. At the rate he was writing, they could be finished by the end of the month—a month ahead of his final deadline. That would give him weeks to go through it and clean it up before sending it on to New York. He was pleased at his progress and he said so.

And when the workday was through, he was his usual sexy, gruff self. By Friday, she'd all but forgotten that something had been bothering him Sunday night.

A week and a day after Addie's baby shower, Elise checked her bank balance online and found that both Sean's and Biff's checks had cleared. Her nest egg was growing by leaps and bounds. She called Jody and they agreed that Jody would keep her eye out for a workable location to lease—or to buy.

That week passed and the one after that. Jed was on the home stretch with *McCannon's Fall*, writing faster and better than ever, he said.

On the last Tuesday in September, Jody called during Elise's lunch break. She had news. The art gallery next to Bloom was closing immediately due to a family emergency. The gallery owner had three months left on her lease, but she wanted out now. Jody had already talked to the agent for the building. He said they would let the gallery owner out of the lease if Elise qualified to take it over. Elise could sign a contract for two years with an option to renew for another two. The agent also said Elise and Jody could open up the wall between the two shops as long as Elise signed a rider agreeing to make all the changes according to code and have the work properly inspected and approved—and to pay a nonrefundable deposit to rebuild the wall at the end of her tenancy.

Jody offered, "I'll pay to fix the wall for us if you put down the nonrefundable deposit."

"Sounds great to me. I've been through the gallery a couple of times. It's a nice space. I'll need to measure it, but I'm pretty sure I can put my kitchen in the back and a little bakery area with a counter and café tables in front."

At the rate Jed was writing, the rough draft could be done within the week. He typed his own rewrites, so he wouldn't need her for that. Maybe she would get lucky and be able to start working for herself again next month.

But even if he needed her right up until November

first, getting the shop next to Bloom for Bravo Catering was as good as it was going to get. Jody wouldn't have to shut down and reopen elsewhere and possibly lose customers in the process. They could build on what Jody already had.

"So are you saying we're going for it?" Jody asked.

"Oh, yeah. I'm in."

After she hung up with Jody, Elise called the agent for Jody's building. He agreed to meet with her on Thursday. Then she called her brother James. Addie's husband was the family lawyer. James said he would go with her to meet the agent.

That settled, Elise still had fifteen minutes left of her lunch break. Time enough to ask Jed for Thursday afternoon off.

She found him just where she expected him to be— in the office looking over the pages he'd written that morning.

He turned in the chair when she came in. "You're early. Eager to get back to work?" It was a joke. She always took the full hour at lunch to rest and recharge for the second half of the workday, which sometimes went past seven at night.

And why was her pulse suddenly racing and her stomach all queasy? All right, when he'd hired her she'd agreed to work all day, every day, six days a week. But surely he could spare her for a few hours on Thursday after more than three months of scrupulous adherence to his killer work schedule.

"Elise?" he prompted when she failed to say a word.

She had to make herself tell him and she hated how hard it was to do that. "I need Thursday afternoon off. The shop next door to Jody in the same building is becoming vacant on the first of the month and I'm going to take it. I need to deal with the owner's agent and get the paperwork going to make it happen."

Jed opened his mouth to remind her that she would be working for him on Thursday afternoon, that she knew very well what the job with him entailed when she took it.

That she damn well was not signing a lease on a space for a shop she was never going to open.

But he knew none of that would fly. She had a right to a day off now and then, no matter what unreasonable demands he'd forced her to agree to when he hired her. The book was a good two weeks ahead of schedule. And even if it hadn't been, his acting like a domineering ass wasn't going to help him convince her that she should stay on with him.

Uh-uh. To get her to stay, he needed to treat her right.

And also to stick with the plan—which was to do nothing until the book was done. So what if she rented a shop? He could pay the lease for her until another tenant came along and took it off her hands. It wasn't a big deal.

"We're ahead," she offered hopefully. "And I'll work Thursday evening if you need me." He rose from his desk and went to her, taking her by the shoulders, running his hands down her arms, linking his fingers with hers. She gazed up at him, apprehension in her eyes.

He squeezed her fingers. "Thursday afternoon is all yours."

Her sweet smile bloomed and she let out a sigh of obvious relief. "Wonderful. Thank you."

"I love it when you're properly grateful." He lowered his mouth to hers and banished all thoughts of her leaving from his mind.

* * *

Elise signed the lease for the shop next to Jody's that Thursday afternoon. She floated on air all the way back to Jed's house.

At dinner, she told him that Jody had already called Nell. Bravo Construction would open up the wall between their two shops and design an attractive iron gate they could close when one shop was open but not the other.

Jed seemed happy for her. He listened to her ramble on about where she might get her kitchen equipment at bargain prices and her vision for the bakery and how much she loved her family.

"The Bravos are really pulling together now," she told him proudly. "For years Nell and I couldn't stand each other and I thought Jody was a snake in the grass. We had all these jealousies, so many simmering resentments, you know? Because my father never could choose between their mother and my mother and essentially he had two families at the same time. We all felt cheated and we took it out on each other. But we've worked through it, united our family. Now, we're always finding reasons to get together. We *like* being together. Nell's got my back and I'd do just about anything for her—and Jody and I are business partners."

He brushed a touch across her hand. "I'm glad it's worked out so well with your family." He really did seem to mean it.

So why did she feel that something was off with him?

Let it go, she reminded herself. *He'll tell you when he's ready.* "So then—shall we work after dinner?"

He gave a low, sexy rumble of laughter. "I can think of better things than work to do after dinner."

They went upstairs early. He drew a bath and they shared it. She surrendered joyfully to the wonder of his big hands on her yearning body.

Had she ever been this happy?

No. Never.

After long months of worry and disappointment, she had everything: enough money, a new business she couldn't wait to make a big success—and most important of all, Jed.

She had love. Real love, deep and true. At last.

Now, if she could just get him to accept that she was moving on professionally...

A week and a day later, Jed got to the end of *Mc-Cannon's Fall*. They went out to dinner to celebrate.

The next day, she asked him if her work on the book was through. He evaded, said he had a few scenes that required serious reworking. He might need her for those.

Monday, he asked her to wait while he "organized the material." He went into his office and he didn't come out all day. That night, when she asked him again if he would need her, he said she should "keep herself available."

And in the morning, he did it again, went into his office to "pull things together" and didn't emerge for hours. When he did come out, he only said he was managing all right on his own "at the moment." He made himself two sandwiches, grabbed a bottle of water and disappeared into his office again.

That night at dinner, she'd had enough of waiting around all day for him to summon her when they both knew he wouldn't need a typist until he started the next book. "Can you just tell me the truth here? You really don't need me on this book anymore."

He took way too long to reply. And when he did, it was only to remind her of what they both already knew. "You're mine until November first. That was the deal."

"Yours. That's an interesting way of putting it."

He shot her a dark glance. "Figure of speech. You know what I mean."

"Yes, I do," she answered gently. "And I *am* yours as a matter of fact. I'm your girlfriend. Your lover. Your woman. All of the above. But as for being your assistant, you really don't need me for that anymore."

"We have an agreement. Until the first of November, *I'll* decide what I need you for."

She looked down at her full plate and realized she had no appetite. "Really?" she asked very softly. "You're going to play the big, bad hard-ass now?"

"November first," he repeated. "That was our deal."

"Jed—"

"I don't want to hear it."

For a moment, she just stared at him as the truth finally sank in: he refused to accept that she needed to move on.

Yep. Dinner for her was definitely over.

She rose, grabbed her plate, carried it to the kitchen and scraped the contents into the garbage bin under the sink. After giving her dish a quick rinse, she put it in the dishwasher and carefully shut the door.

Then she marched back to the table and stood behind her chair. Gripping the back of it, she tried to keep her voice even and calm. "I want to be with you. I think we have something good together. I love brainstorming your work with you. I'm happy to be your sounding board whenever you need one. But I don't want to type for a living. I don't know how to make myself any clearer on that point. I want you to admit that my part of this book is over. I want you to let me go."

He gave her a long, slow once-over. "Let you go," he repeated flatly.

She gripped the chair harder and tossed his own words back at him. "Figure of speech. You know what I mean."

He turned his gaze to his plate again and ate several bites of pork chop stuffing without saying a word. Just when she was considering grabbing her water glass and emptying it over his big, obstinate head, he looked up from his plate and into her eyes. "We need to talk." It was exactly what they needed. So why did she hate the sound of those words? "Sit down, Elise. Please?"

She yanked out the chair and dropped into it.

"I'm sorry," he said, his voice marginally gentler. "I just don't want to lose you."

"But you're not losing me. I'm not going anywhere."

"Yeah, you are. You're going to work with Jody. If you do that, I'm on the hunt for another assistant. And we both know how that's going to go."

She wanted to reach out, put her hand over his, to tell him she loved him and it would all work out. But would it? At the moment, she had her doubts. So she settled for repeating what she'd said way too many times already. "My leaving the job was always going to happen. That was our deal from the beginning. But I will still be here, still be with you, still be yours in the ways that really matter."

He shook his head. "You refuse to see it. You won't admit it. If you go to work with Jody, it *won't* be the way it is now. Until I find someone else I can work with, I'm going to be on edge. It's going to mess up what we have."

"You don't know that. You're in charge of your attitude and your behavior. If you can predict that you're going to act like an ass, then you can figure out a way to behave differently."

"It's not that easy."

"I never used the word *easy*, Jed. I only said that you don't have to ruin what we have because you're frustrated about work."

"Don't you get it?" He pushed the question out through clenched teeth. "I don't *want* another assistant. You're perfect for me in every way. I thought Anna was good, but you are a genius."

"Jed. It's just typing."

"No, it's not. It's everything. The way you listen. The stillness in you when there's a pause. The way you *know*. It's as though you're typing the words before I even say them."

"Thank you. I mean that. But it's just that I'm not intimidated by you, that's all. You'll find someone else who—"

"No, I won't. And I just don't understand why you'd rather be a shopkeeper than my writing partner."

A shopkeeper. She didn't like the way he'd said that, with a sneering curl to his lip and a grunt of disdain. She loved her work. What gave him the right to look down on it? She was seriously tempted to rise from her chair and walk out, just leave him alone with his half-eaten stuffed pork chop and his superior attitude.

But she loved him. So much. Enough to keep trying to get through to him. "Jed. Are you listening to yourself? First off, when it comes to your writing, I'm your assistant, not your partner and—"

"Wait." He put up a hand. "Stop right there."

She blinked and sucked in another calming breath. "Yes?"

"I do have an offer for you. I think it's a pretty good one."

"An offer?" Now he'd totally lost her. "An offer of what?"

"I'm up for contract. It's going to be a big one. If you stay, I'll bring you in as a co-author. You'll get thirty percent of the advance and royalties *and* your name on the next book right under mine."

Elise could only gape. She knew very well how huge it was for him to make her an offer like that. Was she tempted? It would be a *lot* of money. And prestige. She would be famous. Her throat clutched. "Oh, Jed…"

"You're worth it," he muttered gruffly. "Just say yes."

Say yes…

Except that she really *wasn't* tempted. Not at all. She wasn't tempted and it wouldn't be right. "It's not what I want, Jed."

Now he was the one gaping. "Do you have a clue how much money we're talking about?"

"A lot. I get that. But I'm not a writer, Jed. *You* are. And I don't want to be a writer any more than I want to be a typist. I want *you.*" *I love you.* She almost said it, but she couldn't. Not now. Not when the world they'd created together in the past few glorious months seemed to be crumbling. "In the end, it wouldn't work for me, even if you paid me way more than you should, even if you put my name on your books. I'm exactly what you said. A shopkeeper, a party planner, a darn good cook.

I don't want to sit in an office day after day typing up stories. *You're* the storyteller. I want to help you and support you. But I have to have my own work and it's better that we face that now."

"I don't believe this." His eyes were green ice. "I offer you the moon and you say you don't want it."

She was losing him. She felt the loss as an ache in the pit of her stomach, an awful, increasing tightness in her chest. Still, she fought on. She tried to make him see. "It's not right, what you've offered me. It's a bribe, pure and simple, and I don't take bribes. You're shooting yourself in the foot over and over and wondering why you have trouble walking. I don't get why you're so blind, why you won't let yourself see it. You either need to stop being so rough on your assistants that you scare them off, or you need to find a different way. Like maybe figure out why you have this weird typing phobia, or try using speech recognition software."

"I do not have a typing phobia." He spoke so slowly, each word clearly enunciated, sharp as one of his knives. "I know how to type. I don't *want* to type. And I have zero interest in special software. That is not my process."

Oh, she could get good and snippy about now. *He* didn't want to type? Well, neither did she, and hadn't she made that excruciatingly clear?

Keep it together, her wiser self advised, though the hothead within had a whole bunch of not-so-nice things she could say.

No. She would not lose her temper. But damned if she would sit here and listen to him go on about his *process*, as if it was something sacred, something cast in stone.

"I have to say it, Jed. Your process isn't working for you."

"You don't know what you're talking about." It came out in a warning growl.

She refused to let him cow her. "I know a lot more than you're willing to give me credit for at the moment, that's for sure. I know that you're standing in your own way on so many levels. You're so much better than this *process* you keep going on about. We both know that you are. You're the man who held me so tenderly all those weeks ago, who listened without judging, who comforted me while I poured out my long, sad story of all the stupid mistakes I've made. You're the man who treats me like I'm beautiful and does it so well that I feel like a queen. The man who showed me how incredible sex could be, the man who flew me first class to New York City and gave me the time of my life there, the one who backed me up when Biff Townley tried to run a number on me again. You're the man who built Wigs his own catio—even though you claim you hate cats. Why do you think you have to scare everyone away? And why do you make writing your books more difficult than it has to be? Do you somehow think you don't deserve the amazing life you've built for yourself?"

"Enough." He said it way too quietly. She looked in his eyes and saw emptiness. He had shut her out, shut her down. And then he said the worst thing of all. "You should go."

Elise flinched as if he'd struck her.

And then the indignation flooded in. She longed to start shouting, to let him know exactly how destructive and stupid and wrong he was being. She needed to tell him off more than she wanted to draw her next breath.

It just felt so unreal. Impossible, that he would do this, that he would so curtly and coldly throw away all that they had.

On the heels of her fury came tears. They pushed at the back of her throat, begging her to let them fall. *I can't go. Don't make me go. I love you…*

Once again, she hovered on the verge of the big declaration.

But no. Tossing in words of love now wouldn't fix what he'd shattered here.

She gulped the tears back before a single one had a chance to dribble down her cheek. Yes, her heart was breaking. But she was angry, too—worse than angry. Furious. It was not a good time to proclaim undying love.

He was right. She had to go.

Chapter Twelve

An hour later, Elise tossed the last of her stuff in her car.

She went back in to get Wigs, knowing she would find him on the catio. As she went down the stairs, she could hear the driving beat of rock music coming from the workout room.

He isn't even going to come out and say goodbye. Traitorous tears tightened her throat again.

With a low hiss of fury, she gulped them back. She hoped he dropped a dumbbell on his foot, the big lunk.

Wigs sat on his catio, nose to the wire fence, watching several small brown birds, which flew off when she opened the French doors.

"Come on, sweetheart. Time to go."

Wigs remained at the fence, staring off toward the slowly darkening sky.

So she went over there, scooped him up and pressed her face to the warm ruff at his neck. "We are out of here. Now."

He purred for her. She found the low sound somewhat comforting as she carried him back through the house and out the door, pausing only to leave her house key and garage-door remote on the counter in the utility room.

The back stairway to her apartment still smelled of donuts. With Wigs in her arms, she paused on the first step.

And remembered...

Their first time. He'd set her on the kitchen counter and taken away all of her clothes. She'd been shy about the weight she'd put on from eating too many donuts.

And he'd said, "Thank God for donuts."

She'd wrinkled her nose at him, hadn't she? And asked, "What does that even mean?"

"It means the donuts look good on you and you should keep eating them," had been the reply.

Well, maybe she would just do that. Buy a whole box of donuts and eat every last one.

She wanted to kill him.

She wanted to get superdrunk, eat a dozen donuts and start auto-dialing his number.

Drunk dialing on donuts. Did it get any worse?

Forget the donuts for now. She went on up the stairs, sticking her key in the lock, pushing open the door.

Somehow, tonight, the place looked smaller and sadder than ever.

Just keep moving. Do what you have to do. You can have your crying jag later.

She brought everything in and set up Wigs with his box and his bowls, his activity center and his best buddy, the cleaning robot. As soon as she had the bowls filled with food and water, she called Nell.

Her sister had barely said "Hello?" before Elise felt the tears rising again.

"Nellie?" It was all she had to say.

"My God. What's happened?"

"Jed and I…"

"What? Tell me."

She gulped the tears back again. "It's over. That's all. It's over with Jed."

Nellie let out a string of very bad words. "I'll deal with him later. Right now, I'm coming over."

That sounded perfect to Elise. "Good. I'm going downstairs and getting donuts. And I think I have a bottle of tequila around here somewhere…"

Nell arrived fifteen minutes later. She brought Jody. And within the hour, all their other sisters—by blood, of the heart and through marriage—came, too. Clara came, and cousin Rory. And Carter's bride Paige. And Chloe, Quinn's wife. Even Addie, a week from her due date, drove in from the ranch where she lived with James. Addie's grandfather's girlfriend, Lola Dorset, came with her. Everybody brought something to contribute to what Elise proudly called her pity party.

They crowded around the dinky kitchen table, eating donuts and Cheetos, trail mix and Oreos, drinking coffee, tea, juice and soft drinks because Elise never did find the tequila and her sisters had enough sense not to bring liquor when a broken heart was involved.

Elise told them how much she loved Jed. She had no shame. Why should she? Jed had been a complete ass, but that didn't mean she'd stopped loving him. She told her sisters how she'd fallen and fallen and kept on falling until she was all the way in love with him. She also told them that he'd offered her a fortune and her name on his books if only she would stay on as his assistant. "And when I said no, we had a big fight. I said some really tough things to him. And then he told me to go."

Nell threatened to kill him in a gruesome, bloody and painful way—after first removing his testicles. She almost looked like she meant it. And that had everyone laughing. They showered Elise in hugs and support, passed her another chocolate-covered old-fashioned and poured her a fresh cup of coffee.

It didn't heal her sad and torn-up heart, but it definitely helped.

And then Tracy called.

Her lifelong best friend said, "I had this feeling. I was going to text and check on you—but then, I don't know. I just had to call. Is everything all right?"

That brought a fresh flood of tears. Her sisters offered more hugs and tissues. She told Tracy everything, that she was in love with a wonderful man who really had no idea how wonderful he was. "Oh, and I'm in partnership with Jody!" she added. She and Jody high-fived across the table and she quickly told Tracy about the upcoming reopening of Bravo Catering.

Tracy congratulated her on her new business venture. "And about this thing with Jed. You're being noble and sweet and not saying it. But I know you need me. I'm coming home, at least for a few days. We can stay up all night and tell each other everything."

But Elise wouldn't have it. "No way. You have a degree to earn. I miss you and I always will, but I've got backup." She smiled through her tears at her sisters close around her. "I'll see you when you come home for Thanksgiving. We'll talk all night then."

Reluctantly, Tracy agreed.

Two days later, Elise got her final check from Jed. It was more than she expected—the entire amount she would have made had she stayed until the end of October.

A terse note came with it. *Don't argue about the amount. You deserve every penny.* She started to call him, but stopped in mid-dial.

He had taught her so much in their time together, not the least of which was her own worth. Yes, she'd said hard things to him. But they had been true things, spoken with love. And he'd sent her away for it.

A big check and a grumpy two-sentence note was hardly "I love you, Elise. Please forgive me."

So she didn't call. She cashed that check and moved on.

The next day Addie had her baby, a little boy they named Brandon after the baby's natural father, who had died far too young. Elise went to the hospital to meet the newest member of the family. She held the tiny boy in her arms and thought of Jed, wished he'd been there, sent a silent prayer to heaven that he was all right.

At least she had plenty to do. She kept busy working long hours with Jody at their expanded location, planning their social media campaign, ordering the equipment for her kitchen, getting it in and installed, hiring her sister-in-law Chloe to design the front area, to create a cozy little bakery, both beautiful and homey. There would be adorable crystal chandeliers, warm pink walls and cute iron tables with comfy padded chairs. And lots and lots of greenery, courtesy of Bloom.

She found that she was happy, mostly, her life back on track after a long string of setbacks. But her heart did ache. Nights were the toughest. Just her and Wigs alone in the darkness of her tiny apartment. She cuddled him close and longed for Jed, though she felt she couldn't reach out to him, that it wasn't for her to make that move.

She tried her best not to worry about him, all alone with no one to talk to.

Jed was not doing well.

At first, he pushed thoughts of Elise from his mind by burying himself in rewrites, working twenty-hour days, barely pausing to eat, let alone sleep. Ten nonstop days and nights after she left him, he sent *McCannon's Fall* off to Carl in New York.

Without the book to fill his mind, things got bad fast.

His bed was too big without her to hold on to. His fancy house was empty, the damn catio deserted. Sometimes, he thought he heard Wigs meowing. He would wander from room to room, knowing he would find nothing, driven to look for the fur ball, anyway.

After a week of that idiocy, he decided he needed to keep active. He worked out until every muscle jumped and quivered with exhaustion. He threw a lot of knives. He visited the shooting range.

On a Thursday, during the first snowstorm of the season, he took his Range Rover halfway up the mountain, where he and his father used to live.

Temperatures that day stayed well below freezing.

As if he cared how cold it was. He had good gear, rated for arctic conditions. When even the Range Rover could go no farther, he set the brake and got out into the driving snow. He found the trail he knew so well and climbed steadily upward, oblivious to the cold and the limited visibility.

The cabin was still there, locked up good and tight. The shed where his dad had stored their library of books hadn't fared as well. A tree limb had fallen on it, gone right through the roof. Jed felt some satisfaction that at least he'd emptied it out years ago and donated the books to the Justice Creek Library.

He stood on the rough steps that led up to the door and stared at the spot where he'd found Calvin Walsh's lifeless body all those years ago. That was a dark day, the day his father died, the day he saw for the first time that he was completely alone in the world.

It had been snowing that day, too. Tears freezing on his cold cheeks, he'd stared at the big man unmoving on the ground and wondered what he was going to do with himself now. He'd known peace and safety, companionship and mutual understanding with his father. It had always been the two of them, Calvin and Jedidiah, father and son, preparing for the end times, alone against the world.

How would he survive in the big, wide, corrupt, noisy world? He'd had no idea. But he had known that he wasn't staying on that mountain all alone. The end times hadn't come and he needed to learn how to live.

And he'd done that, hadn't he? He'd succeeded beyond his wildest imaginings. He was *the* Jed Walsh, a household name. He wrote the books people wanted to read and he made the big bucks.

But standing there on the steps of the one-room house where his father had raised him, staring at the empty, snowy ground where Calvin Walsh had fallen, he knew he'd gone nowhere.

He was as alone as he'd ever been—no. More so, now that he loved Elise. Now that he knew what it was to look in a woman's eyes and see everything, a full life, that strange thing called happiness, a future filled with laughter and tears, disagreements and compromises, with everything that made it all worthwhile.

The wind sang through the tall trees and the snow kept on falling, covering the rocky ground in pure, cold white. Jed turned and started back down the mountain.

That night and the next and the one after that, he woke in the darkest hours before dawn, disoriented. For a moment or two, he would wonder what was missing. And then he remembered: the woman he loved curled up in his arms. And that damn cat purring from the foot of the bed...

It took those three nights after he went up the mountain for him to finally accept what he needed to do. And it wasn't to find another assistant. He was finished with that. In his life as a writer, he'd found two women capable of putting up with him while he worked. Two women who understood him and took care of him and didn't take any of his crap. One had been like the mother he'd lost too soon.

The other was Elise.

After Elise, no one would stack up. There was no point in torturing even one more hapless keyboarder.

He needed another way. And what else was there for him to do but get going on that? He went into his office and sat down at his desk.

And after three more weeks of working like a madman, he was finally ready to go after what mattered most.

Jed knew where to find her. A few bills and circulars originally addressed to her apartment had shown up in his mailbox after she left and before she'd had them rerouted again. He'd sent that mail on to her—but not before making a note of where she lived.

On the Saturday before Thanksgiving, he got in the Range Rover and headed for Creekside Drive. He parked in the lot in back of her building and entered through the rear door. The smell of donuts hit him, along with a memory so perfect and sweet: Elise on the kitchen counter, shy, breathless and wonderfully soft. He'd never forget that night—or those little pink panties he'd torn off to get to her...

Longing almost doubled him over. He looked up the narrow stairs and didn't know if he could do it.

What if she couldn't forgive him? What if she'd simply moved on?

Didn't matter. He had no choice here. He couldn't go on without at least giving it a shot.

He gripped the banister and started climbing.

Hers was the first door on the right. He knocked.

Nothing. So he knocked again. Still no answer. He peered through the peephole, saw nothing and pictured her on the other side, refusing to answer, peering right back at him.

He tried the doorknob. Locked. He should call.

But he was afraid to call. What if she hung up on him? Surely she'd take pity on him and hear him out if he could only reach her face-to-face.

He went back down the stairs and out the door. Once in the car, he made himself call her.

The call went straight to voice mail. The answering message wasn't even her voice. "You have reached Elise Bravo and Bravo Catering. Please leave a message."

"Elise. I need to talk to you. Please call me back." He disconnected before he realized he hadn't left his name.

It had been almost two months since he'd sent her away.

Could she have forgotten what his voice sounded like in that time? Would she even know it was him?

She would, he realized, because she had his number programmed into her phone.

Didn't she?

He wasn't 100 percent sure...

God. He was pitiful. A hopeless case.

He started up the car and headed home—and somehow ended up on Central Street. And there it was, Bravo Catering, right next door to Bloom. He parked and went in. There were glass cases filled with wonderful-smelling muffins and cupcakes, greenery everywhere and old-timey crystal chandeliers overhead. Half the tables were occupied with smiling, muffin-eating customers. It was charming and well done.

"What can I get you today?" asked the pretty girl behind the counter.

"I want to speak with Elise."

"I'm sorry, you missed her. She's got a wedding today." A wedding? So soon? Didn't women take months and months to plan those? The girl behind the counter smoothed her pink apron. "Just let me take your name and number and—"

"No. It's okay. I'll...get in touch with her later." He turned and started for the door—but then, at the last minute, he pivoted and went under the wide interior arch to Bloom.

Jody turned from watering a fern as he approached. She didn't look especially happy to see him. "Jed Walsh." She marched over and plunked the watering can down on the register counter. "We all thought you died. You're lucky Nellie has restrained herself or you'd be missing a few vital body parts."

Okay, he was a douche. It wasn't news. "You can't possibly despise me as much as I do myself."

"Oh, but I can try. What is the *matter* with you?"

"A lot. Jody, I really need to see her."

Jody's mouth was a thin slash of complete refusal. "She's working."

"The girl in the bakery said she had a wedding…"

"Call her. Leave a message."

"I did. I forgot to leave my name. I… Come on, Jody. I know I don't deserve another chance with her, but give me a break here."

Jody stared at her watering can for an endless count of five, then turned on Jed again. "You want another chance?"

He held out both arms wide. "You are looking at a desperate man. Come on. Where is she?"

"Can't you just wait until—"

"I've waited too long already. Think about it. You'll know it's true. This shop—yours and hers." He gestured at the greenery around them, the bakery through the archway, all of it. Everything. "It's great. Well done. I get it. I know it's what she wants and I want her to have that. Whatever she wants. I know I ruined everything. Just give me a chance to make it right."

Jody eyed him sideways. "She took this wedding at the last minute. An old friend of ours got engaged at Halloween and wanted to have the big wedding *and* do it right away. Leesie's worked her butt off. If you mess it all up by making a scene…"

"No scenes. I swear to you. Just tell me where to find her."

* * *

The friend's wedding was in a farmhouse several miles out of town. Jed parked with the wedding guests, in an open field not far from the house. The snow from three weeks before had long since melted. It was a sunny day, mild for November. He walked up the wide driveway to the front door, where a white-haired lady greeted him, pinned a rosebud to the lapel of his jacket and kissed him on the cheek.

"You've just made it in time." She put a finger to her wrinkled lips. "Shh, now. They're all in the living room." She ushered him inside.

He went through a roomy foyer with a wide, flower-bedecked staircase leading up and on into the living room, where flowers were everywhere and the bride and the groom stood facing a guy in a clerical collar in front of a big brick fireplace.

The white chairs arranged in rows with an aisle down the middle were all occupied. Jed hung back near the arch to the foyer and watched two people he'd never seen before exchange their vows. They did look happy, he thought. And deeply in love.

He remained, staying out of the way as much as possible, through all of it—the picture-taking and the quick, expert switch from row seating for the ceremony to a buffet line and tables for the reception. A four-piece band set up in a corner and began playing dance music.

And Elise?

She was everywhere. She wore a pink cashmere sweater and one of those pencil skirts that clung to every lush, delicious curve. He wanted to duck into a closet and wait for her to walk by—just pop out, snatch her hand, haul her in there and start making up for all the time they'd lost.

But he didn't. He behaved himself. On the drive out here, he'd come up with a plan—not a very good one, true. But the best he could do given that he wasn't going home until he'd had a chance to talk with her. He would stay out of her way until the reception was over. He reasoned that as long as she didn't know he was here, he wouldn't be disrupting the party.

So he kept his eye out, ducking quickly out of sight whenever she got too close or looked as though she might glance his way. It wasn't easy, keeping her from spotting him. She was constantly on the move. She kept track of everything and yet at the same time, she didn't seem to be rushing or under any pressure. She was serene. Unruffled. Even bobbing and weaving to keep her from spotting him, he could see that this was her element.

And that had him worried all over again that he didn't have a chance with her now. Why would she ever come back to a man who'd tried to bully her into giving up the work she loved?

As the guests started filling plates at the buffet, the sweet older lady who'd greeted him at the door took his arm. "I've been trying to place you. Now, let me guess. You're Jerry's cousin Silas, aren't you?"

He made a vaguely agreeable sound that could have meant anything.

"I knew it." The old lady chuckled. "I'm Marlena. So lovely to finally meet you, Silas."

"Marlena, the pleasure is all mine."

She squeezed his arm. "A big man like you? You must be starving."

"Now that you mention it, that prime rib looks amazing." There was a guy in a chef's hat carving a giant, juicy-looking roast halfway down the buffet line.

Marlena let go of his arm and patted his back. "Well, get after it, Silas. And don't be a stranger, you hear me now? I know you and Jerry have had your disagreements, but family is family. Jerry speaks of you often. He misses you terribly."

By then, Jed was starting to feel a little guilty for letting the sweet old lady think he was someone he wasn't. He gave her another grunt of agreement and hit the buffet.

Once he had a plate piled high with prime rib and several mouthwatering sides, he chose a table in the corner, kind of out of the way, with a pillar to duck behind whenever Elise came too close. A couple of guys who were probably at least Marlena's age joined him. The food was delicious—no surprise there, given Elise's talents in the kitchen. And the company was great, too. The old guys, Mervin and Bob, were brothers, WWII vets who'd both been at the Battle of the Bulge. The three of them were talking brilliant military maneuvers through history when Jed smelled clean sheets and knew he was busted.

She was standing right behind him. Dear God, just the smell of her...

Longing coursed through him. She bent close and a loose curl of her hair brushed his cheek. He had to order his grasping hands not to reach back and grab her. "Outside," she whispered. "Now."

When he dared to turn his head, she was already headed for the door. He made his excuses to Bob and Mervin and hustled out after her.

She led him halfway to the field where the cars were parked. Then finally, she stopped and braced her hands on those fine, full hips. "I've seen the guest list. You're not on it."

He kept his arms at his sides, though every muscle yearned to reach for her. "I needed to talk to you. I was going to wait until the party was over, I swear to you I was."

Those coffee-brown eyes got softer—or was that just wishful thinking on his part? "It's not the time, Jed. I'm working."

"I know, but—"

"Look. If you'll call me tomorrow, we can meet, okay? We can talk."

Hope. He felt it now. A feather lightness in his chest, a burning in his brain. He only needed to grab her and kiss her, shove her in the Range Rover and drive away fast. Somehow, he kept himself from doing that. "Tomorrow? I'll call, you'll answer. You mean that?"

Her eyes were softer still. "I do."

His control broke. "Elise." He reached for her.

But she jumped back. "Not here. I mean it. Tomorrow. Please."

It took all the will he had, but he put a lid on it. "Tomorrow. Okay." And he made himself turn and head for his car.

He went back to his house.

But he couldn't stay there. He stopped the car in the garage—and then shifted into Reverse and backed it right out.

Where the hell to now?

He knew where: her place.

* * *

The back door onto the parking lot was locked when he got there. But he went around front, bought a glazed donut and ate it as he wandered down the hallway past the restrooms. The door at the end was unlocked.

Did he feel like a stalker?

Maybe a little.

Too bad. She'd said she would take his call tomorrow. He was only moving the time frame up a little. Nothing wrong with that. He polished off the donut and ducked into the men's room to rinse the sugar off his hands.

When he went back to the hallway, it remained deserted. He went on through the door at the end. Five steps more and he reached the stairs leading up to her apartment.

He went up and sat on the top step to wait.

An hour went by. And another. She still wasn't back.

Well, fine. He would wait all night if he had to.

Eventually, he leaned his head against the wall and closed his eyes. He must have dropped off because he woke up to the sound of a motorboat speeding toward him.

"Wigs. What the hell?" Wigs didn't answer, but the purring got louder. He pulled the cat onto his lap. "She's not going to like finding you out here with me."

Wigs reached up a hairy paw and gently patted his cheek. Jed stroked the thick orange fur. Eventually he leaned his head against the wall and went back to sleep.

The next time he woke, Elise was standing over him. The view was spectacular. But he tried his best to look regretful. "I'm sorry. I couldn't stay away—and I have no idea how this damn cat got out. I was sitting here minding my own business and suddenly he was in my lap."

She shook her head—at him. And at the cat in his lap, too. And then she said something wonderful. "Come on inside."

So he rose and carried Wigs into the one-room apartment. It wasn't fancy and it was much too small. Still, she'd made it cozy, with bright pictures on the walls and comfortable furniture attractively arranged.

"Homey," he said, and it was, because she was there.

She took the cat from him. He waited while she opened a can and filled one of the cat bowls. Wigs dug in. She washed her hands and dried them, took the pins from her hair and shook it out on her shoulders, at which point he realized he would pay half his next advance to be allowed to sift his fingers through the coffee-colored strands.

But first things first. He held up a memory stick.

When she eyed it with wariness, he quickly explained, "This is the first three chapters of my next book. I wrote it using voice recognition software— which I have to admit, has come a long way since the last time I tried it." Did she look doubtful? He couldn't really blame her. "I get that the last thing you want or need right now is an update on Jack McCannon. But still, I'm asking you to bring this up on your laptop. I need you to see that I really did it—I wrote sixty-three pages without terrorizing a single innocent assistant."

By then, those eyes had gone soft again and her beautiful mouth trembled. "I would love an update on Jack McCannon." She whipped the stick from his hand and opened the laptop that waited on the counter. "There's a beer in the fridge. Take another nap. Whatever. I'm going to need at least an hour. Maybe more…"

He did grab himself a beer. But sleeping? No freaking way. He sat on the sofa with Wigs draped along the back of it while she read the material through.

When she turned on her stool to meet his eyes at last, hers were suspiciously misty. "It's good. It's really good. I do have a few suggestions…"

He stood. "And I can't wait to hear them."

"But not right now." She sounded slightly breathless. Breathless was excellent.

"No. Not right now." He closed the short distance from the sofa to the counter. Gently, he guided a curl of hair behind her ear—and she let him. She even leaned a little into his hand. "I went to Bravo Catering today. It's beautiful, what you've done with the bakery. And the wedding? I wasn't even invited and I had a great time. The food was so good. And I watched you."

Did she seem disapproving? A little. He couldn't say he blamed her. She asked, "How long were you there?"

"I lurked for hours, ducking out of sight whenever you got near and I shamelessly pretended to be some guy named Silas."

She laughed. "What in the…? Silas?"

"Long story. Doesn't matter. What I mean is, you were doing what you love to do and you're really good at it and it shows." He caught her hand then, brought it to his lips and kissed it. "Elise, I was so wrong. I can't even count the ways."

Her eyes got misty. "Oh, yes you were. And I was so afraid, Jed. That you would never come for me." A tear escaped then. It left a shining trail as it slid down the velvety curve of her cheek.

He wiped it up with a finger and put it to his tongue—salty. And very sweet. "I couldn't come for you. Not until I knew what to do, how to move forward. And it's been bad, Elise. Now I've been with you, none of it makes much sense if you're not there."

"Oh, I know the feeling."

"I couldn't stand for you to see me like that, desperate and scared. Trapped in a bad place, afraid I would never find my way out."

"But Jed, you saw *me* like that the first morning I made you breakfast."

He ran the backs of his fingers down the side of her throat. Her skin was cool velvet. "I remember that day. You made me French toast. Best I ever tasted."

"And then I burst into tears and ran to my room and you followed me and listened to me pour out my sad tale of woe. You held me and comforted me and...well, you made it all better. I want to be the one who makes all better for you."

He caught her face between his hands, bent down and pressed a kiss against those lips he would never get enough of tasting. "You do make it all better for me."

"But you sent me away."

"I told you. I didn't want—"

"—me to see you like that. I heard you."

"And there's more," he admitted. "It gets worse. After you, there was no way I was having another person in my office sitting in your chair, typing my words for me. No one could compare, that's a simple fact. And then there was what you told me the day I asked you to leave, that I needed to get out of my own way, not be so hung up on my precious *process*. You were so right. Until I did change it up, until I proved to myself that I could make it happen on my own, there always would have been the danger that I would start in on you again, that I would try to manipulate you into typing my words for me, into saving my ass."

She laid her cool, soft hand against his cheek. "I have more faith in you than that."

"How can you? I did try to manipulate you. You told me repeatedly that you were done when the book was done and I refused to believe you." He shook his head and grumbled, "And I can't believe I'm confessing all this. I should keep my mouth shut. Quit while I'm ahead."

"Uh-uh. You should be honest with me. And you are." Her smile bloomed wide. "And I'm so glad. But I do need you to promise me that in the future, if things get bad for you, turning your back on what we have together won't be an option. In the bad times, you have to let me be there for you, no matter how tough it gets for you. That's part of what we are, part of you and me together."

He couldn't make that promise fast enough. "We have a deal. From now on, no matter how bad it gets, we're both staying. Nobody gets away. There's no escape. You're stuck with me."

"Good." She said it so easily, with no hesitation.

He stroked a hand down her hair. "How'd I get so lucky to have a chance with you?"

"Well, you did agree to pay me four thousand a week—and then there was that jetted tub." She was grinning.

And he couldn't let another minute go by without saying it. "I love you, Elise."

Color flooded her wonderful face. "And I love you, Jed."

Words rose in his throat and he let them spill out. "I want to marry you. I want a life with you…" What was he saying? He was babbling like an idiot. He should shut up. But the words just kept coming. "It's too early, right, to be asking you that? And there should be a ring. I know that. A ring with a diamond so big, you can't possibly say no. I've botched it. I can see that. I'm doing this all wrong and I—"

"Jed." She gazed up at him, surprisingly dewy-eyed after all his stupid blathering. "Yes."

The world spun to a stop. "I don't... I can't... Did you just say yes?"

She laughed then, full out and glorious. "Yes, Jed. Yes, yes, yes!"

That did it. He kissed her—a proper kiss. Slow and wet and deep. And then he scooped her up, carried her over to the bed in the corner and got to work undressing her. Once all her beautiful curves were bare for him, he got rid of his own clothes, as well.

They stood together, naked by the side of her bed. "Come home with me tonight, you and the fur ball."

"Yes, we'll come home with you."

"But first..." Taking her shoulders, he guided her down to sit on the edge of the bed. Then he kneeled at her feet. Looking up into her misty eyes, he saw the truth so very clearly. From the day his father died, nothing in the world had really made sense to him. There had been no one who claimed him, no one who felt like his own— not until now. "You're everything to me, Elise. I can't be- lieve I've found you at last, can't believe that you're here, that you said yes, that you're taking me back."

"I love you, Jed." She bent over him, close and then closer. He smelled her fresh scent, felt her breath in his hair, her soft fingers caressing his neck. She urged him up onto the bed with her and held him to her heart. He lost himself in the welcoming heat of her body.

Afterward, she fell asleep in his arms. He didn't want to wake her, so they ended up staying the night in her little apartment.

In the morning, she made him French toast for breakfast. Then she packed up her suitcases and gathered all the cat stuff together. He helped her carry everything down to the cars. She followed him home.

When they got there, before she even brought Wigs in, he took her hand and led her out the open garage door, around to the winding front walk and up the wide porch steps.

"Wait right here." He unlocked the door, stepped in just long enough to turn off the alarm and then stepped back out. She laughed as he swung her high in his arms and carried her over the threshold.

And then she kissed him. "I love you," she said, her dark eyes shining. "I'm so glad you came to get me, Jed. I'm so glad you've finally brought me home."

* * * * *

Watch for Darius Bravo's story
A BRAVO FOR CHRISTMAS
coming in December 2016
only from Harlequin Special Edition.

Single mom Andrea Montgomery only agreed to look in on injured sheriff Marshall Bailey as a favor to his sister, but when these lonely hearts are snowed in together, there's no telling what Christmas wishes might come true.

Turn the page for a sneak peek of
SNOWFALL ON HAVEN POINT
by New York Times *bestselling author*
RaeAnne Thayne,
available October 2016
wherever Harlequin books and ebooks are sold!

CHAPTER ONE

SHE REALLY NEEDED to learn how to say no once in a while.

Andrea Montgomery stood on the doorstep of the small, charming stone house just down the street from hers on Riverbend Road, her arms loaded with a tray of food that was cooling by the minute in the icy December wind blowing off the Hell's Fury River.

Her hands on the tray felt clammy and the flock of butterflies that seemed to have taken up permanent residence in her stomach jumped around maniacally. She didn't want to be here. Marshall Bailey, the man on the other side of that door, made her nervous under the best of circumstances.

This moment definitely did not fall into that category.

How could she turn down any request from Wynona Bailey, though? She owed Wynona whatever she wanted. The woman had taken a bullet for her, after all. If Wyn wanted her to march up and down the main drag in Haven Point wearing a tutu and combat boots, she would rush right out and try to find the perfect ensemble.

She would almost prefer that to Wyn's actual request but her friend had sounded desperate when she called earlier that day from Boise, where she was in graduate school to become a social worker.

"It's only for a week or so, until I can wrap things up here with my practicum and Mom and Uncle Mike make it back from their honeymoon," Wyn had said.

"It's not a problem at all," she had assured her. Apparently she was better at telling fibs than she thought because Wynona didn't even question her.

"Trust my brother to break his leg the one week that his mother and both of his sisters are completely unavailable to help him. I think he did it on purpose."

"Didn't you tell me he was struck by a hit-and-run driver?"

"Yes, but the timing couldn't be worse, with Katrina out of the country and Mom and Uncle Mike on their cruise until the end of the week. Marshall assures me he doesn't need help, but the man has a compound fracture, for crying out loud. He's not supposed to be weight-bearing at all. I would feel better the first few days he's home from the hospital if I knew that someone who lived close by could keep an eye on him."

Andie didn't want to be that someone. But how could she say no to Wynona?

It was a good thing her friend had been a police officer until recently. If Wynona had wanted a partner in crime, *Thelma & Louise* style, Andie wasn't sure she could have said no.

"Aren't you going to ring the doorbell, Mama?" Chloe asked, eyes apprehensive and her voice wavering a little. Her daughter was picking up her own nerves, Andie knew, with that weird radar kids had, but she had also become much more timid and anxious since the terrifying incident that summer when Wyn and Cade Emmett had rescued them all.

"I can do it," her four-year-old son, Will, offered. "My feet are *freezing* out here."

Her heart filled with love for both of her funny, sweet, wonderful children. Will was the spitting image of Jason while Chloe had his mouth and his eyes.

This would be their third Christmas without him and she had to hope she could make it much better than the previous two.

She repositioned the tray and forced herself to focus on the matter at hand. "Sorry, I was thinking of something else."

She couldn't very well tell her children that she hadn't knocked yet because she was too busy thinking about how much she didn't want to be here.

"I told you that Sheriff Bailey has a broken leg and can't get around very well. He probably can't make it to the door easily and I don't want to make him get up. He should be expecting us. Wynona said she was calling him."

She transferred the tray to one arm just long enough to knock a couple of times loudly and twist the doorknob, which gave way easily. The door was blessedly unlocked.

"Sheriff Bailey? Hello? It's Andrea Montgomery."

"And Will and Chloe Montgomery," her son called helpfully, and Andie had to smile, despite the nerves jangling through her.

An instant later, she heard a crash, a thud and a muffled groan.

"Sheriff Bailey?"

"Not really...a good time."

She couldn't miss the pain in the voice of Wynona's older brother. It made her realize how ridiculous she was being. The man had been through a terrible ordeal in the last twenty-four hours and all she could think about was how much he intimidated her.

Nice, Andie. Feeling small and ashamed, she set the tray down on the nearest flat surface, a small table in the foyer still decorated in Wyn's quirky, fun style even though her brother had been living in the home since late August.

"Kids, wait right here for a moment," she said.

Chloe immediately planted herself on the floor by the door, her features taking on the fearful look she had worn too frequently since Rob Warren burst back into their lives so violently. Will, on the other hand, looked bored already. How had her children's roles reversed so abruptly? Chloe used to be the brave one, charging enthusiastically past any challenge, while Will had been the more tentative child.

"Do you need help?" Chloe asked tentatively.

"No. Stay here. I'll be right back."

She was sure the sound had come from the room where Wyn had spent most of her time when she lived here, a space that served as den, family room and TV viewing room in one. Her gaze immediately went to Marshall Bailey, trying to heft himself back up to the sofa from the floor.

"Oh, no!" she exclaimed. "What happened?"

"What do you think happened?" he growled. "You knocked on the door, so I tried to get up to answer and the damn crutches slipped out from under me."

"I'm so sorry. I only knocked to give you a little warning before we barged in. I didn't mean for you to get up."

He glowered. "Then you shouldn't have come over and knocked on the door."

She hated any conversation that came across as a confrontation. They always made her want to hide away in her room like she was a teenager again in her grandfather's house. It was completely immature of her, she knew. Grown-ups couldn't always walk away.

"Wyn asked me to check on you. Didn't she tell you?"

"I haven't talked to her since yesterday. My phone ran out of juice and I haven't had a chance to charge it."

By now, the county sheriff had pulled himself back onto the sofa and was trying to position pillows for his leg that sported a black orthopedic boot from his toes to just below his knee. His features contorted as he tried to reach the pillows but he quickly smoothed them out again. The man was obviously in pain and doing his best to conceal it.

She couldn't leave him to suffer, no matter how nervous his gruff demeanor made her.

She hurried forward and pulled the second pillow into place. "Is that how you wanted it?" she asked.

"For now."

She had a sudden memory of seeing the sheriff the night Rob Warren had broken into her home, assaulted her, held her at gunpoint and ended up in a shoot-out with the Haven Point police chief, Cade Emmett. He had burst into her home after the situation had been largely defused, to find Cade on the ground trying to revive a bleeding Wynona.

The stark fear on Marshall's face had haunted her, knowing that she might have unwittingly contributed to him losing another sibling after he had already lost his father and a younger brother in the line of duty.

Now Marshall's features were a shade or two paler and his eyes had the glassy, distant look of someone in a great deal of pain.

"How long have you been out of the hospital?"

He shrugged. "A couple hours. Give or take."

"And you're here by yourself?" she exclaimed. "I thought you were supposed to be home earlier this morning and someone was going to stay with you for the first few hours. Wynona told me that was the plan."

"One of my deputies drove me home from the hospital but I told him Chief Emmett would probably keep an eye on me."

The police chief lived across the street from Andie and just down the street from Marshall, which boded well for crime prevention in the neighborhood. Having the sheriff *and* the police chief on the same street should be any sane burglar's worst nightmare—especially *this* particular sheriff and police chief.

"And has he been by?"

"Uh, no. I didn't ask him to." Marshall's eyes looked unnaturally blue in his pain-tight features. "Did my sister send you to babysit me?"

"Babysit, no. She only asked me to periodically check on you. I also brought dinner for the next few nights."

"Also unnecessary. If I get hungry, I'll call Serrano's for a pizza later."

She gave him a bland look. "Would a pizza delivery driver know to come pick you up off the floor?"

"You didn't pick me up," he muttered. "You just moved a few pillows around."

He must find this completely intolerable, being dependent on others for the smallest thing. In her limited experience, most men made difficult patients. Tough, take-charge guys like Marshall Bailey probably hated every minute of it.

Sympathy and compassion had begun to replace some of her nervousness. She would probably never truly like the man—he was so big, so masculine, a cop through and through—but she could certainly empathize with what he was going through. For now, he was a victim and she certainly knew what that felt like.

"I brought dinner, so you might as well eat it," she said. "You can order pizza tomorrow if you want. It's not much, just beef stew and homemade rolls, with caramel apple pie for dessert."

"Not much?" he said, eyebrow raised. A low rumble sounded in the room just then and it took her a moment to realize it was coming from his stomach.

"You don't have to eat it, but if you'd like some, I can bring it in here."

He opened his mouth but before he could answer, she heard a voice from the doorway.

"What happened to you?" Will asked, gazing at Marshall's assorted scrapes, bruises and bandages with wide-eyed fascination.

"Will, I thought I told you to wait for me by the door."

"I know, but you were taking *forever*." He walked into the room a little farther, not at all intimidated by the battered, dangerous-looking man it contained. "Hi. My name is Will. What's yours?"

The sheriff gazed at her son. If anything, his features

became even more remote, but he might have simply been in pain.

"This is Sheriff Bailey," Andie said, when Marshall didn't answer for a beat too long. "He's Wynona's brother."

Will beamed at him as if Marshall was his new best friend. "Wynona is nice and she has a nice dog whose name is Young Pete, only Wynona said he's not young anymore."

"Yeah, I know Young Pete," Marshall said after another pause. "He's been in our family for a long time. He was our dad's dog first."

Andie gave him a careful look. From Wyn, she knew their father had been shot in the line of duty several years earlier and had suffered a severe brain injury that left him physically and cognitively impaired. John Bailey had died the previous winter from pneumonia, after spending his last years at a Shelter Springs care center.

Though she had never met the man, her heart ached to think of all the Baileys had suffered.

"Why is his name Young Pete?" Will asked. "I think that's silly. He should be just Pete."

"Couldn't agree more, but you'll have to take that up with my sister."

Will accepted that with equanimity. He took another step closer and scrutinized the sheriff. "How did you get so hurt? Were you in a fight with some bad guys? Did you shoot them? A bad guy came to our house once and Chief Emmett shot him."

Andie stepped in quickly. She was never sure how much Will understood about what happened that summer. "Will, I need your help fixing a tray with dinner for the sheriff."

"I want to hear about the bad guys, though."

"There were no bad guys. I was hit by a car," Marshall said abruptly.

"You're big! Don't you know you're supposed to look both ways and hold someone's hand?"

Marshall Bailey's expression barely twitched. "I guess nobody happened to be around at the time."

Torn between amusement and mortification, Andie grabbed her son's hand. "Come on, Will," she said, her tone insistent. "I need your help."

Her put-upon son sighed. "Okay."

He let her hold his hand as they went back to the entry, where Chloe still sat on the floor, watching the hallway with anxious eyes.

"I told Will not to go in when you told us to wait here but he wouldn't listen to me," Chloe said fretfully.

"You should see the police guy," Will said with relish. "He has blood on him and everything."

Andie hadn't seen any blood but maybe Will was more observant than she. Or maybe he had just become good at trying to get a rise out of his sister.

"Ew. Gross," Chloe exclaimed, looking at the doorway with an expression that contained equal parts revulsion and fascination.

"He is Wyn's brother and knows Young Pete, too," Will informed her.

Easily distracted, as most six-year-old girls could be, Chloe sighed. "I miss Young Pete. I wonder if he and Sadie will be friends?"

"Why wouldn't they be?" Will asked.

"Okay, kids, we can talk about Sadie and Young Pete another time. Right now, we need to get dinner for Wynona's brother."

"I need to use the bathroom," Will informed her. He

had that urgent look he sometimes wore when he had pushed things past the limit.

"There's a bathroom just down the hall, second door down. See?"

"Okay."

He raced for it—she hoped in time.

"We'll be in the kitchen," she told him, then carried the food to the bright and spacious room with its stainless appliances and white cabinets.

"See if you can find a small plate for the pie while I dish up the stew," she instructed Chloe.

"Okay," her daughter said.

The nervous note in her voice broke Andie's heart, especially when she thought of the bold child who used to run out to confront the world.

"Do I have to carry it out there?" Chloe asked.

"Not if you don't want to, honey. You can wait right here in the kitchen or in the entryway, if you want."

While Chloe perched on one of the kitchen stools and watched, Andie prepared a tray for him, trying to make it as tempting as possible. She had a feeling his appetite wouldn't be back to normal for a few days because of the pain and the aftereffects of anesthesia but at least the fault wouldn't lie in her presentation.

It didn't take long, but it still gave her time to make note of the few changes in the kitchen. In the few months Wynona had been gone, Marshall Bailey had left his mark. The kitchen was clean but not sparkling, and where Wyn had kept a cheery bowl of fruit on the counter, a pair of handcuffs and a stack of mail cluttered the space. Young Pete's food and water bowls were presumably in Boise with Young Pete.

As she looked at the space on the floor where they

usually rested, she suddenly remembered dogs weren't the only creatures who needed beverages.

"I forgot to fill Sheriff Bailey's water bottle," she said to Chloe. "Could you do that for me?"

Chloe hopped down from her stool and picked up the water bottle. With her bottom lip pressed firmly between her teeth, she filled the water bottle with ice and water from the refrigerator before screwing the lid back on and held it out for Andie.

"Thanks, honey. Oh, the tray's pretty full and I don't have a free hand. I guess I'll have to make another trip for it."

As she had hoped, Chloe glanced at the tray and then at the doorway with trepidation on her features that eventually shifted to resolve.

"I guess I can maybe carry it for you," she whispered.

Andie smiled and rubbed a hand over her hair, heart bursting with pride at this brave little girl. "Thank you, Chloe. You're always such a big help to me."

Chloe mustered a smile, though it didn't stick. "You'll be right there?"

"The whole time. Where do you suppose that brother of yours is?"

She suspected the answer, even before she and Chloe walked back to the den and she heard Will chattering.

"And I want a new Lego set and a sled and some real walkie-talkies like my friend Ty has. He has his own pony and I want one of those, too, only my mama says I can't have one because we don't have a place for him to run. Ty lives on a ranch and we only have a little backyard and we don't have a barn or any hay for him to eat. That's what horses eat—did you know that?"

Rats. Had she actually been stupid enough to fall

for that "I have to go to the bathroom" gag? She should have known better. Will had probably raced right back in here the moment her back was turned.

"I did know that. And oats and barley, too," Sheriff Bailey said. His voice, several octaves below Will's, rippled down her spine. Did he sound annoyed? She couldn't tell. Mostly, his voice sounded remote.

"We have oatmeal at our house and my mom puts barley in soup sometimes, so why couldn't we have a pony?"

She should probably rescue the man. He just had one leg broken by a hit-and-run driver. He didn't need the other one talked off by an almost-five-year-old. She moved into the room just in time to catch the tail end of the discussion.

"A pony is a pretty big responsibility," Marshall said.

"So is a dog and a cat and we have one of each, a dog named Sadie and a cat named Mrs. Finnegan," Will pointed out.

"But a pony is a lot more work than a dog *or* a cat. Anyway, how would one fit on Santa's sleigh?"

Judging by his peal of laughter, Will apparently thought that was hilarious.

"He couldn't! You're silly."

She had to wonder if anyone had ever called the serious sheriff *silly* before. She winced and carried the tray inside the room, judging it was past time to step in.

"Here you go. Dinner. Again, don't get your hopes up. I'm an adequate cook but that's about it."

She set the food down on the end table next to the sofa and found a folded wooden TV tray she didn't remember from her frequent visits to the house when Wynona lived here. She set up the TV tray and transferred the food to it, then gestured for Chloe to bring the water bottle. Her daughter hurried over without meeting his gaze, set the bottle on the tray, then rushed back to the safety of the kitchen as soon as she could.

Marshall looked at the tray, then at her, leaving her feeling as if *she* were the silly one.

"Thanks. It looks good. I appreciate your kindness," he said stiffly, as if the words were dragged out of him.

He had to know any kindness on her part was out of obligation toward Wynona. The thought made her feel rather guilty. He was her neighbor and she should be more enthusiastic about helping him, whether he made her nervous or not.

"Where is your cell phone?" she asked. "You need some way to contact the outside world."

"Why?"

She frowned. "Because people are concerned about you! You just got out of the hospital a few hours ago. You need pain medicine at regular intervals and you're probably supposed to have ice on that leg or something."

"I'm fine, as long as I can get to the bathroom and the kitchen and I have the remote close at hand."

Such a typical man. She huffed out a breath. "At least think of the people who care about you. Wyn is out of her head with worry, especially since your mother and Katrina aren't in town."

"Why do you think I didn't charge my phone?" he muttered.

She crossed her arms across her chest. She didn't like confrontation or big, dangerous men any more than her daughter did, but Wynona had asked her to watch out for him and she took the charge seriously.

"You're being obstinate. What if you trip over your

crutches and hit your head, only this time somebody isn't at the door to make sure you can get up again?"

"That's not going to happen."

"You don't know that. Where is your phone, Sheriff?"

He glowered at her but seemed to accept the inevitable. "Fine," he said with a sigh. "It should be in the pocket of my jacket, which is in the bag they sent home with me from the hospital. I think my deputy said he left it in the bedroom. First door on the left."

The deputy should have made sure his boss had some way to contact the outside world, but she had a feeling it was probably a big enough chore getting Sheriff Bailey home from the hospital without him trying to drive himself and she decided to give the poor guy some slack.

"I'm going to assume the charger is in there, too."

"Yeah. By the bed."

She walked down the hall to the room that had once been Wyn's bedroom. The bedroom still held traces of Wynona in the solid Mission furniture set but Sheriff Bailey had stamped his own personality on it in the last three months. A Stetson hung on one of the bedposts, and instead of mounds of pillows and the beautiful log cabin quilt Wyn's aunts had made her, a no-frills but soft-looking navy duvet covered the bed, made neatly as he had probably left it the morning before. A pile of books waited on the bedside table and a pair of battered cowboy boots stood toe-out next to the closet.

The room smelled masculine and entirely too sexy for her peace of mind, of sage-covered mountains with an undertone of leather and spice.

Except for that brief moment when she had helped him back to the sofa, she had never been close enough to Marshall to see if that scent clung to his skin. The idea made her shiver a little before she managed to rein in the wholly inappropriate reaction.

She found the plastic hospital bag on the wide arm-chair near the windows, overlooking the snow-covered pines along the river. Feeling strangely guilty at invading the man's privacy, she opened it. At the top of the pile that appeared to contain mostly clothing, she found another large clear bag with a pair of ripped jeans inside covered in a dried dark substance she realized was blood.

Marshall Bailey's blood.

The stark reminder of his close call sent a tremor through her. He could have been killed if that hit-and-run driver had struck him at a slightly higher rate of speed. The Baileys likely wouldn't have recovered, especially since Wyn's twin brother, Wyatt, had been struck and killed by an out-of-control vehicle while helping a stranded motorist during a winter storm.

The jeans weren't ruined beyond repair. Maybe she could spray stain remover on them and try to mend the rips and tears.

Further searching through the bag finally unearthed the telephone. She found the charger next to the bed and carried the phone, charger and bag containing the Levi's back to the sheriff.

While she was gone from the room, he had pulled the tray close and was working on the dinner roll in a desultory way.

She plugged the charger into the same outlet as the lamp next to the sofa and inserted the other end into his phone. "Here you are. I'll let you turn it on. Now you'll have no excuse not to talk to your family when they call."

"Thanks. I guess."

Andie held out the bag containing the jeans. "Do you mind if I take these? I'd like to see if I can get the stains out and do a little repair work."

"It's not worth the effort. I don't even know why they sent them home. The paramedics had to cut them away to get to my leg."

"You never know. I might be able to fix them."

He shrugged, his eyes wearing that distant look again. He was in pain, she realized, and trying very hard not to show it.

"If you power on your phone and unlock it, I can put my cell number in there so you can reach me in an emergency."

"I won't—" he started to say but the sentence ended with a sigh as he reached for the phone.

As soon as he turned it on, the phone gave a cacophony of beeps, alerting him to missed texts and messages, but he paid them no attention.

"What's your number?"

She gave it to him and in turn entered his into her own phone.

"Please don't be stubborn. If you need help, call me. I'm just a few houses away and can be here in under two minutes—and that's even if I have to take time to put on boots and a winter coat."

He likely wouldn't call and both of them knew it.

"Are we almost done?" Will asked from the doorway, clearly tired of having only his sister to talk to in the other room.

"In a moment," she said, then turned back to Marshall. "Do you know Herm and Louise Jacobs, next door?"

Oddly, he gaped at her for a long, drawn-out moment. "Why do you ask?" His voice was tight with suspicion.

"If I'm not around and you need help for some reason, they or their grandson Christopher can be here even faster. I'll put their number in your phone, too, just in case."

"I doubt I'll need it, but...thanks."

"Christopher has a skateboard, a big one," Will offered gleefully. "He rides it without even a helmet!"

Her son had a bad case of hero worship when it came to the Jacobses' troubled grandson, who had come to live with Herm and Louise shortly after Andie and her children arrived in Haven Point. It worried her a little to see how fascinated Will was with the clearly rebellious teenager, but so far Christopher had been patient and even kind to her son.

"That's not very safe, is it?" the sheriff said gruffly. "You should always wear a helmet when you're riding a bike or skateboard to protect your head."

"I don't even *have* a skateboard," Will said.

"If you get one," Marshall answered. This time she couldn't miss the clear strain in his voice. The man was at the end of his endurance and probably wanted nothing more than to be alone with his pain.

"We really do need to leave," Andie said quickly. "Is there anything else I can do to help you before we leave?"

He shook his head, then winced a little as if the motion hurt. "You've done more than enough already."

"Try to get some rest, if you can. I'll check in with you tomorrow and also bring something for your lunch."

He didn't exactly look overjoyed at the prospect. "I don't suppose I can say anything to persuade you otherwise, can I?"

"You're a wise man, Sheriff Bailey."

Will giggled. "Where's your gold and Frankenstein?"

Marshall blinked, obviously as baffled as she was, which only made Will giggle more.

"Like in the Baby Jesus story, you know. The wise men brought the gold, Frankenstein and mirth."

She did her best to hide a smile. This year Will had become fascinated with the small carved Nativity set she bought at a thrift store the first year she moved out of her grandfather's cheerless house.

"Oh. Frankincense and myrrh. They were perfumes and oils, I think. When I said Sheriff Bailey was a wise man, I just meant he was smart."

She was a little biased, yes, but she couldn't believe even the most hardened of hearts wouldn't find her son adorable. The sheriff only studied them both with that dour expression.

He was in pain, she reminded herself. If she were in his position, she wouldn't find a four-year-old's chatter amusing, either.

"We'll see you tomorrow," she said again. "Call me, even if it's the middle of the night."

"I will," he said, which she knew was a blatant fib. He would never call her.

She had done all she could, short of moving into his house—kids, pets and all.

She gathered the children part of that equation and ushered them out of the house. Darkness came early this close to the winter solstice but the Jacobs family's Christmas lights next door gleamed through the snow.

In the short time she'd been inside his house, Andie had forgotten most of her nervousness around Marshall. Perhaps it was his injury that made him feel a little less threatening to her—though she had a feeling that even

if he'd suffered *two* broken legs in that accident, the
sheriff of Lake Haven County would never be anything
less than dangerous.

Available October 18, 2016

#2509 A CHILD UNDER HIS TREE
Return to the Double C • by Allison Leigh
Kelly Rasmussen and Caleb Buchanan were high school sweethearts until life got in the way. Now they're both back in Weaver and want a second chance, but everything is made more complicated by the five-year-old little boy with his secret father's eyes.

#2510 THE MAVERICK'S HOLIDAY SURPRISE
Montana Mavericks: The Baby Bonanza • by Karen Rose Smith
Trust-fund cowboy Hudson Jones wants Bella Stockton, but day-care babies and a secret stand in their way. Can Hudson help Bella overcome her intimacy fears—and can Bella convince the roaming cowboy that home for the holidays is the best place to be?

#2511 THE RANCHER'S EXPECTANT CHRISTMAS
Wed in the West • by Karen Templeton
When jilted—and hugely pregnant—Deanna Blake returns to Whispering Pines, New Mexico, for her father's funeral, single dad Josh Talbot sees everything he wants in a partner in the grown-up version of his old friend. But how can this uncomplicated country boy heal the city girl's broken heart?

#2512 CALLIE'S CHRISTMAS WISH
Three Coins in the Fountain • by Merline Lovelace
Callie Langston is *not* boring! And to prove it, she's going to Rome to work as a counselor to female refugees over Christmas. Security expert Joe Russo learned the hard way how cruel the world can be when his fiancé was murdered, and he plans on making sure Callie is protected—always. Even if that means he has to follow her halfway around the globe. But can Callie's thirst for adventure and Joe's protective instincts coexist long enough for her Christmas wish to come true?

#2513 THANKFUL FOR YOU
The Brands of Montana • by Joanna Sims
Dallas Dalton wants to mess up city-boy lawyer Nick Brand's perfectly controlled exterior from the moment they meet. Nick can't explain why he's drawn to the wild-child cowgirl, he just knows he is. But they come from completely different worlds, and it might just take a Thanksgiving miracle to prove to them they have more in common than they think.

#2514 THE COWBOY'S BIG FAMILY TREE
Hurley's Homestyle Kitchen • by Meg Maxwell
Christmas is coming and rancher Logan Grainger is struggling with the news that another man is his biological father. He recently became guardian to his orphaned nephews and learned that his new nine-year-old stepsister is being fostered by his old flame Clementine Hurley. She wants them to be a family, but can Logan move past the lies to bring them all together under a Christmas tree?

YOU CAN FIND MORE INFORMATION ON UPCOMING HARLEQUIN® TITLES, FREE EXCERPTS AND MORE AT WWW.HARLEQUIN.COM.

"Why do you care, Caleb?"

He was silent for so long she wasn't sure he was going to answer. And since he wasn't, she pushed away from the brick. "I need to get back to Tyler."

"I've always cared."

His words washed over her. Instead of feeling like a balmy wave, though, it felt like being rolled against abrasive sand. "Right." She stepped around him.

"Dammit." His hand shot out and he grabbed her arm. She tried to shaking him off. "Let go."

"You asked and I'm telling you. So now you're going to walk away?" He let her go. "I swear, you're as stubborn as your mother."

She flinched.

He swore again. Thrust his fingers through his dark hair. "I didn't mean that."

Why not? She adored her son. Didn't regret his existence for one single second. In that, she was very different from her mother. But that didn't mean she wasn't Georgette Rasmussen's daughter with all the rest that that implied.

"I have to go." She tried stepping around his big body again.

"I'm sorry that I hurt you. I was always sorry, Kelly. Always."

She looked up at him. "But you did it anyway."

"And you're going to hate me forever because of it? It was nearly ten years ago!"

When he'd dumped her for another girl.

And only six years when she'd impetuously, angrily put her mouth on his and set in motion a situation she still couldn't change.

Which was worse?

His actions or hers?

Her eyes suddenly burned. Because she was pretty sure keeping the existence of his own son from him outweighed him falling in love with someone far better suited to him than simple little Kelly Rasmussen.

He made a rough sound of impatience. "If you're gonna hate me anyway—"

She barely had a chance to frown before his mouth hit hers.

Don't miss
A CHILD UNDER HIS TREE by Allison Leigh,
available November 2016 wherever
Harlequin® Special Edition books and ebooks are sold.

www.Harlequin.com

EXCLUSIVE
Limited Time Offer

$1.⁰⁰ OFF

New York Times bestselling author

RaeAnne Thayne

There's no place like Haven Point for the
holidays, where the snow conspires to bring
two wary hearts together for a Christmas
to remember.

SNOWFALL ON
HAVEN POINT

Available September 27, 2016.
Pick up your copy today!

HQN™

$7.99 U.S./$9.99 CAN.

$1.⁰⁰ OFF the purchase price of SNOWFALL ON HAVEN POINT by RaeAnne Thayne.

Offer valid from September 27, 2016, to October 31, 2016.
Redeemable at participating retail outlets. Not redeemable at Barnes & Noble.
Limit one coupon per purchase. Valid in the U.S.A. and Canada only.

52613933

Canadian Retailers: Harlequin Enterprises Limited will pay the face value of this coupon plus 10.25¢ if submitted by customer for this product only. Any other use constitutes fraud. Coupon is nonassignable. Void if taxed, prohibited or restricted by law. Consumer must pay any government taxes. Void if copied. Inmar Promotional Services ("IPS") customers submit coupons and proof of sales to Harlequin Enterprises Limited, P.O. Box 3000, Saint John, NB E2L 4L3, Canada. Non-IPS retailer—for reimbursement submit coupons and proof of sales directly to Harlequin Enterprises Limited, Retail Marketing Department, 225 Duncan Mill Rd., Don Mills, ON M3B 3K9, Canada.

5 65373 00076 2 (8100)0 12185

U.S. Retailers: Harlequin Enterprises Limited will pay the face value of this coupon plus 8¢ if submitted by customer for this product only. Any other use constitutes fraud. Coupon is nonassignable. Void if taxed, prohibited or restricted by law. Consumer must pay any government taxes. Void if copied. For reimbursement submit coupons and proof of sales directly to Harlequin Enterprises Limited, P.O. Box 880478, El Paso, TX 88588-0478, U.S.A. Cash value 1/100 cents.

PHCOUPRAT1016

THE WORLD IS BETTER WITH

Romance

Harlequin has everything from contemporary, passionate and heartwarming to suspenseful and inspirational stories.

Whatever your mood, we have a romance just for you!

Connect with us to find your next great read, special offers and more.

f /HarlequinBooks

🐦 @HarlequinBooks

www.HarlequinBlog.com

www.Harlequin.com/Newsletters

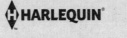

H HARLEQUIN®

A *Romance* FOR EVERY MOOD™

www.Harlequin.com